I0763552

# ANTHOLOGY OF SCROLLS

## SHORT STORIES, POETRY & PROSE

P.A. WIKOFF

All stories edited by Crystal Wikoff. Copyediting by Cheryl Wikoff. He Came First additionally edited by Laurie Gibson.

A very special thanks to Christy Allen for some sweet, sweet beta reading!

Cover artwork by Marcela Bolivar. Copyright ©2017/2018
All photographs taken by P.A. Wikoff except the Eiffel Tower picture (which was taken by Crystal Wikoff).

Check out:
Pawikoff.wordpress.com
@pawikoff on twitter & Instagram
Facebook.com/pawikoff
Marcelabolivar.com

ISBN: 0-9990058-1-2
ISBN-13: 978-0-9990058-1-1

# AUTHOR'S NOTE

I've run into many authors, big and small, who begrudgingly admit to writing "angsty poetry." They always have to preface it by adding the word "phase" to justify such a time in their lives that has long since passed.

Never one for reading, writing, or anything to do with poetry, I too once turned my nose up at the notion. The perception I had of myself was that of a "fantasy writer" only. And if it weren't for the many literary journals and various contests that I participated in, that perception would have remained intact.

During this process of expanding myself, I learned that I enjoyed writing outside my own image as much as and in some cases more than in my genre of choice.

Each one of the twenty-eight stories in this anthology involves a piece of myself or a problem that I was trying to slay. Writing has inherently become my own personal therapy session, with myself acting as both the therapist and the couch warmer.

As for poetry in particular, it was a hard hurdle for me to overcome. But once I did, it didn't matter what the words said or the way they were laid out. In the end, I found that I just felt better on the subject. It was as if transferring my feelings to the page made them lose all power over me.

So, like other authors before me, this might be my "angsty poetry phase" or it might just be me. In either case, I am proud that I made it out the other side, from the blankness that follows "The End" and on to another adventure, changed for the better.

# CONTENTS


| | |
|---|---|
| THE LIBRARIAN'S STORY | 1 |
| FALLING | 28 |
| TRI-ANGER | 36 |
| HE CAME FIRST | 38 |
| POCKETS VOID OF GREEN | 45 |
| THEY WERE NEVER YOU | 48 |
| BE CALM | 96 |
| THE OTHER SIDE OF BORROWED TIME | 99 |
| IN THE NAME OF THE CHUMP | 107 |
| HEAVEN CAN WEIGHT | 110 |
| HE STARES AT ME | 115 |
| THE LONELY POISON | 117 |
| CIRCLES | 131 |
| ILLITERATE SPELLING | 133 |
| HERE WE GO AGAIN | 193 |
| OBSOLETE | 195 |
| FORGOTTEN FLOWER | 222 |
| OUT OF MY MIND | 225 |
| BROKEN | 253 |
| AN UNDESERVING MAN | 256 |
| BATWOLF | 271 |
| ESTRANGED | 275 |
| A NIGHT TO FORGET | 277 |
| BACKPEDALING THROUGH TIME | 284 |
| DEAD SIRIOUS | 286 |
| THE NOTE TO MYSELF I'LL NEVER READ | 304 |
| CUT IN HALF | 308 |
| 'TIS THE TREASON | 310 |
| ABOUT THE AUTHOR | 316 |

# PUBLICATIONS

Batwolf – First published on 404words.com
He Stares at Me – First published on Fiftywordstories.com
A Night to Forget – First published on Prose.com
Out of My Mind – First published in After Effects
Falling – First publish on The Monkey Collective

# THE LIBRARIAN'S STORY

Everyone calls me "Crazygirl," a name that is completely unfounded I promise you. But when you don't have a birth name, you accept the first alias that is given to you...and "Crazygirl" is mine. As far as I know, mental illness isn't prominent within my family—not that I remember any of my family, or my past for that matter. Let me start at the beginning, or at least the beginning for me.

I awoke just like every other human being, confused, crying and completely naked, with only one exception—I was already an adult. I didn't suppose I had just launched out of my mother in some way, though I looked around contemplating the unrealistic possibility nevertheless. No, there would have been amniotic fluid and a whole lot of other business, if that were the case. Forgetting my indecent predicament, I chuckled loudly at my own foolishness on the matter.

Can you imagine how large of a bulge a pregnant woman would have if she held a fully reared adult inside her? Forget about ever wearing heels again. She would need a wheelbarrow, or at least an auxiliary set of legs to carry the load. Birthing a thing roughly the same size as yourself would surely rip you in half. I know I'm not the first person who has ever contemplated such an event. Isn't that the whole premise for the Russian dolls? One inside another, inside another... Even the toy makers knew that one had to be cut in half to let out the slightly smaller Russian doll inside. I imagine it like a stripper popping out of a giant cake at a bachelor party, where the cake is another slightly larger person. I'm sure that no one would cheer or pay to see such a display, no matter how miraculous of an event it might be.

Also, if I were merely an adult-sized baby, I wouldn't know things and have sagacious thought.

A catcaller's loud wolf whistle interrupted my train of thought, and I launched behind a parked car to regain my modesty.

*Where are my clothes? Why do I care if I have any or not?* I looked around at the bustling sidewalk where people were mostly too self-involved with their own importance to notice a streaker failing at concealing all her bits.

If I were a man, or had a third arm, I might be able to cover myself completely. However, the extra appendage might draw in more unwanted attention.

Hiding behind a car had prevented any traffic accidents from occurring and sheltered me from the foot-traffic on the other side of the street. However, this being a three-dimensional world, my hiding spot didn't block me from the pedestrians on *this* side of the street.

I wondered if the car I was bare-bottomed against was unlocked. I glanced at the elevated position of the door lock. I was positively sure, well, fairly certain...almost convinced that, maybe, it might be open. Trespassing inside someone else's property was a crime of substance, or maybe just a slap on the wrist? In either case, I might find myself the proud new owner of an orange jumpsuit if I happened to get caught, which sounded pretty okay right about now.

It was the leering scowl and licking lips of a homeless man that forced my hand to squeeze the door handle and enter the vehicle.

The funny thing about car alarms is that they can be set even if the door locks are not. The blaring noise shattered my eardrums, drawing in even more attention to my uncomfortable predicament.

Have you ever smelled the rancid stench of a skunk's spray? Not just while in the car driving home from a Sunday at grandma's house. I mean really smelled it—like you got sprayed in the face, or your dog was hit, and he rubbed the putrid stuff all over the couch. In the frontlines of the skunk's biochemical warfare, the aroma seems unnatural and somewhat synthetic. The very first time I'd encountered the rancid plume, I thought there was an electric fire, or maybe I was having a stroke. If you know what I'm talking about, you'll see where I'm going with this. If you don't, you should pick a fight with one of these striped bandits then return to the story for a better grasp of the analogy.

It's similar with car alarms. They are loud and annoying from afar, but horrifyingly dreadful up close.

Scrambling around in the back seat, I felt like a caged animal—part of some science experiment, or worse. My fingernails started to dig into the budget upholstery. With a cheerful chirp and two flashes of the car lights...it finally stopped. It was as if the car was saying, "My bad."

Then I saw the owner of the sedan with his outstretched arm holding the key remote...and he was coming this way. I got down low, hiding myself in the foot space of the backseat. With my eyes shut and covered by my hands, I tucked into myself. *I am a ghost.* I had to rely on my ears to describe the current events for me, as I wouldn't dare to try and sneak a peek.

The door flew open, without care or concern for the hinges. The engine started up eagerly and he revved it twice. The economy vehicle wasn't up for the type of reckless driving his heavy foot suggested. The radio picked up exactly where he had left it—a rhythm and blues track, which he started to sing off key at the top of his lungs. He had no rhythm, and it was giving me the blues. I moved my hands from my eyes to my ears. *Maybe that alarm wasn't so bad.*

His driving was erratic and spastic—starting fast and braking even faster. He turned the wheel like it was a video game. I even caught him making his own engine noises in between music tracks. It was evident that it was only a matter of time before we both were burned alive in a fiery crash. My only saving grace was that I didn't have any clothes to act as kindling if that were to happen.

This had to end. While at a stoplight, I got enough courage to unravel myself slowly like a snake. I peeked over the seat to spy him singing to himself in the rearview mirror.

"You are my hero, forever and..." he broke off mid song, noticing the naked woman ominously creeping up on him. He instinctively hit the gas while turning his head completely around. His scream was endless. At least his frightened tone was one steady note, which was better. Only now, he wasn't watching his own bad driving—which surprisingly was the same.

I tried to calm him down by placing my finger over my lips, but it only made things worse. He swatted at me with an effeminate swing, now taking both hands off the wheel. I had inadvertently predicted and caused my own death.

Forgetting about my bashfulness, I leaped over him and grabbed ahold of the wheel. It was either his fear or total shock that I was in the buff that caused him to faint into my bosom. I pushed his body off mine, hoping it would dislodge his foot from the accelerator, but it didn't. I decided to embrace fate and just drive.

With his foot still on the gas, I navigated the low-trim-level vehicle, stretching from the backseat. The sad thing was, I think I was doing a better job than he had, even without the use of the brake pedal.

Getting comfortable, I rested my elbow on his head and started to relax. If it wasn't for red lights it might have actually been an enjoyable experience.

Driving over a speed bump, his foot slid off the gas. Then, the sedan started to slow to a crawl, and I tucked into a parking spot.

I reached to turn the key off when the driver abruptly awoke with the same energy he had had before. "Get the hell out of my car, you Crazygirl!"

Startled, I scrambled out of the backseat and onto the quiet street lined with quaint storefronts. I didn't know where I was or what I was to do. I causally walked away, only now I didn't hide my misfortune—I walked with my shoulders and head held high. I could still hear the vituperation of the driver as he drove away.

Every shop seemed to be dark and closed—even before the setting sun had clocked out for the day. My step quickened. A newspaper took flight as the wind kicked up the very moment I took interest in it. The more I chased the parchment, the more it danced and taunted my failure. My first intention was to read the date, but now it was personal.

I chased it like a cat with a string—intense and agile, caring only for the chase. Down the block and through an alley, I tracked the thing until I cornered it in a stone doorway. I pounced on the paper, instantly shredding it. Regretting what I had done, I tried to piece it back together. I felt a warm draft against my bare skin. It was coming from an open door.

I took a moment to appreciate the stone gothic architecture of the library I was standing before. I don't recall my feet ever moving, though before long, I was inside. The library had arched ceilings and smelled of antiquity. Old leather-bound books lined every inch of the place, and large ladders were built to access the high shelves. Knowledge burst out of the bindings, almost begging to be absorbed. For such a relic, the décor was in mint condition and completely dust-free. I could have sworn I heard whispers, yet there wasn't a single soul inside the ancient building. I quickly closed the front door, hoping it was the echoes of the outside. I felt at home, like a cold cavewoman finally finding her cave.

On the front desk there was a sign, "Please check in/out your own books and pay your own fees. $.10 a day for overages. The librarian is on vacation."

There was no one around to ask permission, so I asked myself, "May I stay and fill the position?" I bowed, accepting my own request. I picked up the sign and crumbled it into a ball.

I spent my first night reading a luculent tale of princes and princesses, and my dreams continued the tale where the book left off.

In the morning, I awoke to the sound of a bell ringing in an agitated manner. Sunlight colored the stained-glass windows and illuminated the room. Before my eyes could adjust, I noticed the oil from my lantern had leaked onto a book from last night's adventure. Everything about this place seemed to be from another era, and without a modern flashlight to accompany my late-night reading, I had almost inadvertently set the place ablaze.

Being so entrenched in the previous night's story, I had forgotten to remedy my indecency problem. Luckily, I had a couple of large books resting next to me, one of which was a mammoth of a dictionary, which held possibly every word in the English language. The tome managed to cover from my chest to my knees as I galumphed sideways over to the desk.

"Why are you walking like that?" a gruff man asked, impatiently waiting at the front desk.

"Bunions," I said with a yawn.

"Bunions?"

"I mean bedsores."

"Huh?"

"What I mean to say is that I read a lot, in bed, and I'm sore. Thus the walk."

"Did I wake you up?" he said, ringing the bell again. Not in an annoyed way, but like a child who couldn't help but mess with things.

"How may I help you, sir?" I asked, arriving at the desk.

"This book is late," he said, sliding over a large volume whose cover was completely rubbed off.

"It looks much worse than that."

"Just take care of it for me, okay?"

This was my first day on the job, with my first customer, and I already caught a snarky one. "What do you want me to do about it, turn back time? If I had a time machine, I could also talk to your mother about teaching you to keep to your agreements once made," I said, taking my new role quite seriously.

"What? No, that would be insane. Are you crazy, girl? I just want to pay the fine."

"By all means. It's ten cents a day."

"That's the thing. I had this book for quite a while, and it was a nickel a day when I checked it out. I don't think I should have to pay the new prices. It's a bait and switch, a scam, a fraud," he stammered, while talking quickly. This was usually a sign of someone who was trying to pull a fast one.

In the background, the hissing sounds of whispers started to echo through the halls like carbonation evacuating slowly out from under a bottle cap, though we were the only two people around.

"I see. How many days late are we talking here?"

"Uh...6,673 and one-half day. Do you count today?"

"Of course we do. It's not as if someone else can borrow it while it's in your possession, can they?"

"I guess it's 6,674 days, then."

"Are you aware that's well over eighteen years?"

"Look, I didn't come here to get ridiculed. I came to pay my debt to society!"

"That'll be $667.40. Would you like to pay by cash or check?"

"Wait a minute, I don't have that kind of money. And when did you raise your rates? Weren't you going to give me a deal, for at least half of it?"

"They could have raised the rate from a nickel to a dime the day after you checked out this book. I wasn't here, so I cannot attest to that happening or not. How about I knock off the forty cents and call it an even 667?"

The mysterious whispering sounds had grown so loud that they were causing me to raise my voice in order to project over them.

"This is outrageous!" He was becoming quite fractious.

"Shhh!" I turned around with a threatening eye, and the room fell silent after my voice stopped echoing off the stone floors.

"Are you without clothes?" the man whispered.

I had nowhere to run, nowhere to hide. I was so wrapped up in my duties, I had forgotten about my breezy outfit...or lack thereof. "You are in no position to judge. This book is in horrible condition, I shouldn't even be taking it back," I deflected, trying to fight the redness that was heating up my face.

"Why don't you...oh, never mind. I have a proposition for yo..."

Before he could finish his sentence, my hand came out of nowhere, like lightning, striking his cheek with a crack.

Thunderous rage was building in his veins as his eyes bugged out of his skull. He was getting ready to burst with emotion.

Before things could get any worse, I was quick to point at the tiny sign on the desk that said, "Quiet, please," with a sketch of a mouse sleeping in a matchbox.

He breathed in deeply, trying to calm himself down before speaking. "I didn't mean like *that*, you crazy girl," he said through his gnashing teeth.

"I'm sorry for that. I'm feeling a little bit vulnerable right now, and you caught me at an awkward time. It was very unprofessional," I said, hiding more of myself behind the slipping dictionary.

"What I was going to say was that my grandmother has a chest of old garments in my attic. How about I bring them to you and we call it even?"

"You want me to dress like your old gran? I would rather have the money." I objurgated him with a scowl.

The man took a sideways glance around the library. "Even if I had the money to pay, you still have no clothes to go out shopping in. Am I right? If you don't like her taste, you can alter them to your liking, or at least leave this place."

He had a point. I needed clothes more than I needed money. The man seemed nice enough to trust that he wasn't going to back out of our deal, or worse, call his friends over to gawk and stare. What other choice did I have? "Ok, fine. But no tricks, mister," I said, with a wag of my finger.

The man quickly turned away, not giving me an opportunity to change my mind.

"Wait! You can't leave this here." I held the late book out to him.

"But I thought we had an agreement. I really need to return this book today," the man said, doubling back to me, defeat resting on his shoulders.

"You can leave the book when you pay the fine and return with the garment." *I can't let him just drop the book off, never to return.* It was policy, or at least it seemed like the logical way to deal with the situation.

"Okay, I'll be back. I promise," the man said, snatching the book from my grasp.

While waiting for my sole customer to return, I perused through a section of ancient books. They were so old that they were without titles or author names embossed on their spines. No codes or tags indicated that they were part of the failproof Dewey

Decimal system.

I approached the oldest book of the lot—its spine was cracked like broken glass. What treasures this old tomb must have held. My eager palms started to moisten with anticipation. I slid the fabric-bound book off the shelf. I breathed in its ancient aroma, which took me back to a forgotten time. It was magnificent. I cracked open the binding, and the brittle pages crumbled inside my hands.

"Oh, no!" Before I could stop from unintentionally destroying a piece of history, the pages had turned completely to dust. My feeling of grief grew deeply as I mourned the loss like it was a cremated friend or loved one. Sometimes our desires take us to the bottom of a dark abyss, and all we can do is look up for forgiveness and guidance. I reminded myself that I can't always have everything I want, but I must want only what is manageable. It was a feasible concept of controlling my lust for abundance.

"I am careless." From what I had seen, nothing written within these walls was jejune. Each volume held a certain level of excellence and wonder, which I'd grown quickly to expect.

My curiosity was a little stronger than the guilt I felt, and I continued to the newest looking of all the old books, eager to digest its works. I held my air inside me, as I pulled the golden-bound book off the shelf. I cracked open the spine. It creaked and groaned like an old door slowly opening. Luckily, the pages were intact. The words were handwritten in a beautiful script. I squinted and strained, trying to make out the words, which were blurry and abstruse. It was clearly written in English, but I couldn't for the life of me seem to read it. I had thought my vision was perfect, but currently it wasn't the case.

*Wait, I was reading smaller-print books last night with no problem.* I looked up at the rest of the room which appeared crystal clear. I observed my own hand, thinking maybe I was far-sighted. *Nope, it isn't me. It's the book.* Something wasn't right. I brought the text in, touching my nose. It seemed to be getting worse the closer I got.

"Hello? I'm back with the goods." I heard the customer return.

I quickly stashed the golden-bound book where it had previously rested.

Awaiting my arrival was a wooden box with fabric poking out like a groundhog out of a hole. The man was turned away from the desk, giving me some much-deserved privacy.

"That was quick," I said, rummaging through the dust-ridden clothes, coughing from the plumes.

"Like I said before, I need to return this book as soon as possible. So, are we good?"

I dug through the junk for a third time, almost losing hope of finding anything that wasn't rife with holes or dust. "Hold on, let me make sure this one fits." I suddenly pulled out a dark, vintage dress with a fringed neckline and puffed shoulders. It reminded me of something out of a story resting on these shelves. Too gorgeous to be overlooked, yet it almost was. I slipped it over my bare skin. It fit snugly and made me feel enchanted, almost powerful, like a bon vivant. My eyes turned watery. It was special, and so was I.

Never expecting to find something so spectacular, I now saw the old box as a treasure chest, and I ravenously searched through the rest of the contents.

"Can I turn around now?"

Tearing through stained scarves and scratchy nightgowns, I responded to him like an animal with a sound I had never made before.

"Wow, did you find that in there?"

"Isn't it wonderful?"

"I could have sworn that dress wasn't in there before. I went through it myself."

I paused and took a second to ponder what exactly he was getting at.

"Not that I had any reason to go through it. What I mean to say is that it's yours."

A genuine smile overtook my face as I continued my task. Reaching the bottom of the box, I pulled out an exquisite necklace. "Is this her? Your grandmother, I mean," I asked, looking at the porcelain portrait carved on the choker.

"I think so. I never knew her to be that young," the man admitted.

"She is beautiful."

"Yeah, she was. You kind of look like her, actually."

I gave him an inquisitive look, wondering if he was flirting with me.

"I mean in a crazy sort of way," he said, noticing my reaction.

I put on the choker, and it made me feel safe as it pressed against my neck.

"Lovely. You can have that too, I suppose."

"I wasn't asking."

He raised a finger as if he had more to say on the matter, though I ignored it and walked over to his book, pulled out the card from the inside flap, and quickly stamped the return date onto it. "Congratulations, your book has been returned."

He took a moment, taking in my image, before he let out a sigh of relief. "Well, I guess I can get on with the rest of my life now." He held himself differently, somehow more relaxed, as if a huge weight had been lifted off his shoulders. Who knew that the lateness of a book could cause such stress with an individual, but here was proof standing in front of me.

"Would you like to check anything else out?"

He waved his hands back and forth, "No, no. I think I'll destroy my library card when I get home. Obviously, I cannot be trusted with the thing."

I looked down at the title of the book he had returned. "The Mirror Inside. Never heard of it. Is it any good?" When I got no answer, I looked up to find that he was already gone, without even a fond farewell. I guess he had somewhere to be. It must be good if he kept it for so long.

I opened it to the first page and found a hand-drawn picture of a small boy, with a small caption typed below, "His hard-earned grades were profitable on this warm summer day. His mother's promise proved true as she handed him a card of infinite knowledge and substance. The words came to him as he read, and his imagination was vast and everlasting."

As I flipped through the pages, I realized that this read more like a diary than any fiction I knew. Each chapter had a sketch similar to the one of the first page, setting the scene for the text to follow. Mundane details were described alongside emotional tornados. I was both fascinated and impatient while weeding through the thousands of pages. I finally skipped to the page before the end. The sketch was still of the boy, only now he was completely grown up. He had the same smug look as he did on the first page, except now I recognized him as the customer who had returned the book. I looked up to where he had once stood, in total amazement.

Outside, I heard the sound of a car screeching its wheels against the pavement, followed by a loud thud.

Fixated on the book, I read the caption aloud, "I never figured out if I was reading the book or it was reading me. My years of confusion and torment ends soon, as I spotted a light on inside the library last night. Hopefully it isn't too late. I feel that it may be, though I am happy to be wrong, as my life is on the line. Her vacation is over."

*Am I missing something? What was his urgency?* I flipped through the previous pages, and found no clue as to what he was referring to. Anxious and bemused, I proceeded to the last page. There was a sketch of a car accident. The shock took my breath as I quickly read the caption, "He went outside, thinking he had rid himself of the curse, but it was only beginning. He had foreseen his own demise...or had the book? In either case, it came true, like every other page in the old book. When he had checked in the book, he had checked himself out of existence. Everything must come to an end sometime. When your hands tire of flipping the pages, when your lungs are tired of pushing air. Without an end, there would be no new starts."

I thought about rushing outside to help the man, but I was more scared about confirming the book's words rather than debunking the theory.

Reluctantly, I turned another page to see how it all ended. I saw a sketch of myself looking back at me. It shared my feeling of horror, as if it were a mirror, though it didn't move. Words started to appear on the page in my own handwriting. "The librarian reads the caption aloud, disbelieving what she is seeing. Is this real or a flaw in her imagination? A dream or a nightmare? She knows there is only one way to find out...she will have to turn the next page."

I swiftly slammed the book closed with a "nope." Looking at the code on the spine, I made my way to the 100's or "Philosophy and Psychology section" of the library.

"I'm not falling for that one, magic or not." *Everyone wants to know the future, until they realize that we all die in the end. It's better to forget how tragic life can be and start capturing moments. Then hold on to them long enough to escape yourself, maybe just for a little while.*

I found the open spot where the book used to rest. Old cobwebs had taken up residence in its absence. I pushed the book back into place, though it was being blocked by something else. It was much too big to be a spider, wasn't it? A chill came over me, as if a spider was crawling up my spine. Putrid thoughts of rodent bones were on the tip of my mind. Never one for overcoming my fears, I decided to cast the book aside, leaving it on the aisle floor. Though there was something far more terrifying about that book than any dead rodent. Something I wasn't about to delve into to appease my curiosity.

Without warning, a new thought washed over me like the tide washes over the sandcastle you spent all morning constructing. *I don't recognize any of the books inside this library, not in this mysterious section, nor the normal ones.*

This didn't just apply to titles, but authors as

well. To test my memory, I rattled off a bunch of famous writers, some of the greatest literary minds history had discovered. Looking through Dewey's system, I found my assumption was correct; none of the greats were listed here.

This discovery was very peculiar indeed, and if I were someone else, I might have pondered it for some time. Something odd was going on, and I eerily fit in like a puzzle piece from a separate set—it completes the scene, but nothing looks or feels exactly right.

Maybe it was in my best interest to return the book to its home, so as not to upset this library or any specters that may or may not have been watching over me that very instant. Just because I didn't believe in such nonsense didn't mean that it couldn't be true. I mean, I didn't believe in daylight savings, but I still set my clock back just the same.

I went back to the "scary shelf" and slowly reached my hand through the cobwebs into the deepest, darkest, evilest part. I felt something hard touch my hand. "Bones, I knew it!" I quickly jerked my hand out of the hole, knocking what I thought was rodent remains to the ground.

After getting up enough nerve to open my eyes, I found that they were only a pair of non-threatening, round-framed glasses. All my fears vanished like a ghost with a rigorous haunting schedule, and I crammed the book back into its rightful place.

The old spectacles were much too grimy to see

through, so I took them back to the front desk and used some old rags from the wooden box to clean off the lenses. They were made from a thick glass, maybe quartz or crystal. Either way, they felt misplaced, almost out of this realm.

I positioned the specs upon my nose, and everything appeared blurry. Knowing for a fact that I had removed all the dust and debris, I figured that they must not be my prescription. Then I noticed something spooky, strange, and a little unsettling. Not everything in my line of vision was blurry. One book looked clear, even from down the aisle. "Andre Fairchild," I read the spine from more than thirty feet away. The letters formed as if I were seeing a phantasm manifesting.

I quickly slid the glasses back, pinning my hair like a headband. The Fairchild book I had just read was now blurry, whereas everything else was crisp with detail. As I made my way to the book, I realized that it was the same golden book I had picked up before—the one with the blurry text. Something was peculiarly wrong with this whole library. There were too many coincidences that were much too convenient to be real. I felt as if some higher force was laughing at me, like I was a rat running through a circular maze.

I felt my heart pounding through my neck as I reached for the book and snapped it open. I saw the exact same blurry text. Nothing had changed. Then I remembered that the glasses were still in my hair.

I pulled them down, and my hair got caught around the nose pads. "Ouch."

It took me longer than it should take one to untangle themselves from wire-frame glasses. Mostly it was due to the excitement inside my fingers. If I had only slowed down, it would have taken half the time for sure.

Finally, I returned the glasses to my face, and as I had feared, the text was now perfectly clear. I sat down cross-legged and immersed myself inside its pages, front to back. It was a wonderful fictional tale of ancient Egypt. It was the most realistic work I'd ever read on the subject, vivid and descriptive. It seemed like a real first-hand account of events I'd never heard of.

Once I finished, I felt more connected to the characters than any book I had ever read. It wasn't about the stories, per say. It was more about how they made me feel. The characters' feelings were like my own. Every plot decision aligned perfectly with how I would have handled the obstacle, even the tragic ones.

After reading the golden-bound book, I felt as though I was changed in some way—wiser and more reserved.

Elated, like a child at a carnival, I ran through the aisles of towering books, looking for another blurry one. That couldn't have been the only one. There had to be more hidden among the literature.

Just as my heart had desired, the universe eventually complied with my request, and I found the next blurry title. Like the first one, I had to rely on my lenses to decipher its meaning. "Romance of the Heart." This work was even more glorious than that first golden book. It was filled with pleasure and delectation—a love story, pure and true. As the lead fell in love, so did I. Her feelings were my feelings. It felt so real within my imagination, as if it were my own past. I drizzled the pages with real tears as we wept together. I wished that it were all true. I would have gladly given up myself and this life to enjoy a single day within these pages—to live in a world so exciting and momentous. I never wanted it to end.

But it did end, and then began my sorrow. I was miserable wondering what my life would have been like if I had never experienced such a masterpiece, if I never chased that newspaper, or got inside that parked car, or worse, never woke up naked in the busy streets of the city. That world was better than living, better than any lifetime could produce. I wished that I could live between the pages and reclaim my heart, which was trapped inside chapter five.

I had to find more.

Racing through the sections, the books whispered at me, and I ignored their taunts. Nothing seemed strange, not anymore. The abnormal had become normal and finding answers to the unknown became less important somehow. I only cared about feeling again—something, anything. Just a little more, even a taste would suffice.

It was a huge undertaking, but I decided that I would have to read every piece of work inside this mysterious treasure to find the gold. Even the non-blurry books were excellent within their genres, though they didn't leave me with the same evolutionary feeling afterwards.

Days melded together as I took book after book off its shelf. It was an immortal feeling. Each page seemed to extend my life as I got lost within the margins—as if life was on pause in this timeless endeavor. I couldn't tell you how many days or months (or more) went by. The only way I could judge was by the huge stacks of books that were scattered around the library.

It was right around the time I feared losing myself completely that I found a third book. I was quite reluctant to open the thing, fearing that I would inevitably reach the end. I contemplated everything—how that strange customer who returned the book inadvertently led me to the magical glasses. What did it all mean? Or was there even any puzzle to solve?

I didn't know how or why, but somehow, I felt that reading this third book would give me all the answers I desired.

I put on the glasses. "The Librarian's Story."

Like a cliff diver throwing all caution to the wind, I dove deeply into the story. I read each word out loud so as to enjoy the story twice as much—once in my mind and the other while my ears heard my own voice. There was something familiar about this particular story.

Like before, I instantly started to experience the glorious feeling that I had from the previous two volumes. Only this time, I felt my emotions pulling at me from all directions. They were from characters in the other books that I had read. Then the mystery all started to unravel, page by page.

*A book without a reader is merely a piece of paper, slowly turning into dust. It's the reader that lends the words their power. They give the words their tears and emotions. It isn't the great writer who takes you on a journey. It's your own imagination that takes the story for a ride, with the words acting as a guide. This is how all books are so subjective. It if weren't for the reader's interpretation, words would remain meaningless. Just symbols on thin sheets of pulp.*

Being solicitously immersed in the story, I couldn't pry my eyes off the text, even though the pages were ripping out of their bindings and swirling around me like a literary cyclone. Scrolls poured off the shelves and became animated, like flying snakes. Something magical was happening, and I would ignore it to finish the tale, even if it would result in my own demise. Indulging in this work was like taking a break from reality, a well-deserved vacation you never want to end.

Upon reaching the final page, I achieved total

enlightenment. Though I may not have had a memory of my past, it was my emotions that had been locked within these pages. I knew now that I had loved and lost, been happy and hurt, and had a whole life filled with a multitude of experiences, and the parchments that swirled around me were a diary of those experiences. It was no longer important for my mind to remember, because the pages had led me there. It was a blueprint of my heart, disguised in verse, like a lover's song imprinted on a scratched record. Ignore the words, and embrace the tragedy.

The scrolls were now leading me somewhere else as the churning pages went towards some place new...

I looked up to see the one thing more mystical than that of the text. It was never written in any book, because mere words couldn't capture its feeling. What was once chimerical was now ethereal—it was the unknown, and it was fresh. I embraced it with an open palm as my body lifted off the ground. I had no idea where I was going, or what I'd see when I got there.

*I promise you one thing, if I come out of this alive, I'll put it in a book. Or at least an anthology of experiences, carving out my emotions with the sharpness of words.*

"Never be afraid of something spectacular. Only fear missing it completely." -The Crazygirl

The End

# F A L L I N G

I believe that I'm the sole reason for the world's destruction. It may sound quite far-fetched or even super egotistical, but the proof is undeniable.

As a small boy, I worshiped hanging around at the shoe and ankle level of adults, diving for pieces of food before the five crucial seconds were up or the dogs got them.

I always knew what the fully-grown members of society were talking about, not based on their words, but by merely watching their legs move. A bashful girl shifts from side to side when she talks to a man she finds attractive. A steady, wide stance is always had by the businessman who aims to "talk a little shop" and close a deal. The insecure guy leans against the wall, on display like a piece of art. We can't always mask our feelings—you just have to look for the signs.

I used to think it was a coincidence that everything always came tumbling down around me, and not just food. Until people started to take notice, they deemed me eccentric or referred to me as a "klutz"—the man with two left feet.

It wasn't like they saw something I didn't. Every single shower was met with the same routine. My elbow would knock the soap out of its slippery dish. When I'd try to bend over and get it, another bathroom essential often came crashing down, hitting my back or head—razors, shampoo, conditioner, you name it.

Without any tests or scientific proof, I blamed my problem on my equilibrium. Was I sick? Did I have an ear infection? *Doubtful.* Could it be something more serious, like cancer? *Most definitely.* Even though I was undiagnosed, I felt like my days were running away from me. I had to slow down and find meaning with each step forward, because it could be my last.

Never one for sports, I used to think the Olympics were a pointless competition. So much sacrifice and hard work for a gold, silver or bronze medal you can't even melt down. That was until I saw the ski jump competition. My stomach twisted and turned when they went up, almost like a phobia. The higher they rose, the worse I felt. Only when they came crashing down did my feelings change to a sort of euphoria. I'd heard of people having a fear of heights because they are afraid of the fall, but I'd never heard of anyone having a fear of heights because they may never come down.

Speaking of fear, remember the big California earthquake...you know, the one where half the state moved east, and every time you travel, one of those tragic, shake-fearing people manages to find you.

"I used to live in California!" they always boast, as if it were the same as living in New York City.

Then you follow up with the same old question, "Why'd you leave?"

I've talked to a ton people and the answer is always exactly the same, "That big earthquake, oh, mama-jamma."

Okay, maybe the "mama-jamma" part isn't verbatim, but inside my mind, I like to embellish the story some, since I've heard it more times than pennies in a dollar. At any rate, the shifting tectonic plates freaked them out enough to pack all their worldly belongings, never looking back.

Speaking of looking back, I just realized that I went off on a tangent. I do that sometimes. So...during the big California earthquake, my cocker spaniel leapt out of my sleeping arms and ran into the den. I got up to see what had upset him, moments before the big one hit. Glassware shifted, books jumped off their shelves, but most importantly, a heavy mirror came crashing down on the exact spot where I had lain my head moments before.

Some might think the dog was psychic, or maybe more in tune with nature's signs. I, for one, knew better. Things were always coming down around me, only this time it was all at once. I felt horrible for all the destruction I'd caused. Almost everyone I knew had cracks in their walls and fallen chimneys. The earthquake was a pivotal part of my childhood because it helped me realize that I needed to become a "fixer" and make amends for any falls that I might inadvertently create.

I learned construction, mechanics and engineering. I even studied religions and spirituality in order to find an answer to my ever-growing question, "What does it all mean?"

If I couldn't figure out why, then I had to get used to hard labor in making reparations. I had racked up well over 2,000 community service hours, without a crime to justify the punishment. Like a roller coaster, with every up, there's a down. This concept also works in reverse. When something came down and I helped put it back, it made me feel up—as if I were high on adrenalin.

My life made sense the moment I started to piece everything together. The signs were always there, just hidden like years-past Easter eggs, and finding them was just as unpleasant. Once I found the correlation, I started to point myself in its direction as if it were my destiny—breadcrumbs leading me to unravel the secrets of the universe.

Even my favorite season is fall. Living in California, we never really get a good, old-fashioned leaf mutiny. All the seasons seem to blend into each other, with the occasional rainstorm. I remember visiting my grandparents on the East Coast when I first set eyes on this spectacular season—piles of leaves for jumping and crunching, the wonderful array of colors in the tan and brown spectrum. Watching the leaves parachute to the ground was just so peaceful. It was like snowfall, though not nearly as cold.

Like most people, I favored my birthday over most days. My entire life, I worshiped November 9, 1989, because it was my day and no one else's. As I grew older, I realized there might be other people in the world who shared November 9$^{th}$ as a birthday (19 million people, last time I checked). Later, I discovered that, as the world's population grew, so did the amount of people born on *my* day. That wasn't the only tidbit; it appeared that the fall of the Berlin Wall also happened at the exact same time I was coming into this world.

I'm not paranoid, it *is* an epidemic...a lifestyle that I've learned to cope with, almost like a reflex. The world is falling apart, and I'm the only person able to put it back together again.

Last spring, I spent a day at Niagara Falls (on the Canadian side, which is much better). As I watched the roaring white water churn and crash, all my thoughts were washed away. I stared at the beautiful sight like a statue, engulfed in the simplistic pleasure of it all. A three-dimensional painting that nature had created for me. I was trapped there, without the will to move. Only the retreating sun gave me the strength to pry myself away from the power it had over me.

Some might think of me as being extremely unlucky, but I see it quite the opposite. Who else do you know that has been involved in two airplane emergency landings and lived to talk about it? Still not convinced? My car was hit by lightning twice in the same year. I was in New York City when the World Trade Center was attacked. I've caught twelve pop fly baseballs without even trying. I keep an extra change of clothes in my truck due to the sheer volume of birds that poop on me. I've only gone to Las Vegas twice, and in both cases a casino was reduced to rubble. Once, they exploded the Aladdin and the other time they blew up the Stardust. These weren't planned visits, just coincidences.

My whole life has been conditioning, honing my defensive skills.

Now, you can only imagine how natural it was for me when I caught her. She was trying to take a photo of herself and lost her footing. I didn't notice her until the camera slipped out of her hands. It was as if she fell into my world. If it weren't for my instincts, she inevitably would have fallen 984 feet, squashing the tourists below.

We were on top of the Eiffel Tower.

But she didn't fall, not far, anyway—just a couple short inches, softly into my arms. We looked at each other breathlessly, holding on to each other like we were the only real things left in the world.

Her angelic smile was pure and beautiful.

My whole life had been preparing me for this one, defining moment. Every other time, things had fallen around me. This was the first and only time I fell for someone else...and she caught my breath.

The End

## TRI-ANGER

Click, Click, Click
I watch the time slip away

Drip, Drip, Drip
I leak from my dismay

Crunch, Crunch, Crunch
I stuff my mouth to block the words

Punch, Punch, Punch
Off the face of the nerds

Clip, Clip, Clip
I try to look like something new

Whip, Whip, ...
I could only handle two

# HE CAME FIRST

Bright lights almost blind his fluttering eyes. The crowd falls silent, in wait, watching him, judging his every move. He wonders what he has done to amass such an audience, studying them as much as they him. Paralyzed with fear, he moves slightly, just to see if he can. Gasps fill the room as if they're stealing all the air out of it.

*What did I do wrong? Are they going to hurt me if I do it again?*

A giant of a man approaches with a "there you have it" sort of gesture. The man is bald, and his self-importance shows clearly in every step. The giant's booming voice echoes deeply, leaving his words muffled, and their meaning escapes him. The crowd is hanging on his every word, every motion.

Thinking they're distracted by the giant, he takes a step closer toward the darkness.

Silence falls over the room for a second time. He did it again—he has their attention. He hates their judging eyes. He feels as if they are cooking him with desire.

"Stop looking at me!" he speaks.

The room laughs uproariously at him, shaming fingers, and jiggling stomachs.

He can't take any more. He flees toward the darkness off stage. A tall cameraman blocks his exit with a squatting stride and open arms. He runs in the other direction, but the bald giant is already blocking his path. With a firm grip, the giant grabs him by the back of the neck.

His heart is pounding through his pulsating veins. He bites the giant's hand, then slides through his legs.

More laughter ensues, to the point where everyone in the audience seems to be having trouble breathing. If he keeps this up, they all might end up dead.

He takes off, up the center aisle, as the chuckling people's hands claw at his body. Pushing through them all adds to the excitement of the day.

He manages to get past them and into the open lobby. He can no longer hear their mocking cries. He can only assume they have met their end from self-indulgent glee.

Straightening himself out, he tries to leave the room casually. He nods at a woman sitting behind the desk. Horror spreads over her face as she quickly reaches for the phone. There is no way he will be able to make it past the security guard next to the door—not at this rate, anyway.

The woman's eyes are tracking his every step while she whispers to the person on the other end of the line, covering her mouth with a cupped hand.

*It is now or never.*

His feet take flight, and he makes a break for the door. All he can hear is the jingling sound of a security guard's keys, who is quick to chase him.

*Why does everyone want to harm me?*

He dodges back and forth. Luckily, the security guard is slightly overweight and rarely has to move his body this much in a normal day.

Thinking he's bold, he runs toward the outside world, following the light. He crashes directly into the large glass window, leaving a grease mark from his head. Everything hurts as the world spins like a top.

*How did I not see that?*

Six people stand above him with interrogating eyes. Six of them turn into four, then two—the woman and the guard. They have kind faces, no longer scared of him. Their gentle hands help him to his feet.

*Maybe this is all a misunderstanding,* he thinks. He smiles at their kindness, feeling calm again.

They both look past him; their endearing eyes turn vacant like the others'. He turns around to see the balding giant coming his way.

"No, not this again!" he says.

The woman and guard both cannot keep themselves from laughing.

He wonders if he has some sort of sickness that is causing this irrational behavior. He doesn't want them to die too, so he pushes forward—this time at the door and not the window.

He is free; he is out. Nothing can stop his stride as he bobs and weaves through the pedestrian traffic on the busy sidewalk.

"I did it!" he yells, catching unwanted attention from everyone within earshot.

Remembering what happened in the lobby, he slows down and takes his time.

He is walking in the shadows of a mother and her two children. The little ones can't stop looking behind them, whereas the mother pretends to ignore him altogether.

His legs can't help but gain on them. When he is nervous, his actions match his heart, and in this instance, it's nearly racing. As he gets closer, the mother pulls in her brood, tucking them under each arm.

One of the little girls holds out a hand with a piece of her snack inside, with a sweet smile. Feeling hungry, he reaches for it. The mother protectively, smacks the snack out of her daughter's hand. She now raises her arm high above her head, ready to strike him if he dares to come any closer to her young.

*Everyone has gone crazy today.* Scrambling, he gets as far away from the family as he can before he feels the other side of her hand.

He knows that he has to lie low. Noticing someone leaving a restaurant, he brushes past their legs and takes a seat inside. No one is looking at him anymore. He starts to breathe easy again.

*Maybe there is something in the air.*

Starving, he picks up some fallen cornbread crumbs on the floor and swallows them whole.

A voice behind the counter yells at him. He looks up at the angry man who has a crazed look to him, like he wants to do bad things to him...unspeakable things.

His eyes slowly slide away from the man behind the counter to the images on the menu wall.

Me?! They're serving *me* as meat. "Cannibal!" he screeches, now knowing what that look was all about. That man has killed before, and he will surely kill again.

He runs out of the open door, certain that the man is going back for his knife to chop him up into little bits and serve him with rice.

*What about this is okay? Why are people acting as if this is normal? Can they not see the carnage openly displayed in broad daylight?*

Knowing he has to keep running, he looks around for another option, any option.

He spies the bald giant coming down the road to his right. To his left, the security guard is talking to the mother and listening to her damning testimony.

There's nowhere to go but to the other side of the road. What other choice does he have? Over there is a park, with birds chirping and squirrels holding the trees down.

The traffic is deadly, and faster than his eyes can follow.

Everyone is descending upon him from all sides. He cannot decide which lunatic would offer him a swifter death.

Fight or flight...he chooses flight.

Running into traffic, he dodges left and right. The cars show no mercy. The blissful sounds of the park are replaced by horns and the revving of these automotive death machines. He feels as if the animals are watching him, encouraging his act of defiance.

Nearly there, he can taste victory. A side-view mirror collides with his back, causing him to tumble to the pavement. His heart pounds inside his chest. He cannot breathe; he cannot anything. Nothing is moving. It is over.

The bald giant towers above him and claps three times.

His perception changes as if waking up from a bad dream. He now remembers the giant's words, which he had forgotten. "Until I clap my hands three times, you will remain a chicken."

Why did he ever try to cross that road?

The End

## POCKETS VOID OF GREEN

I can't afford to eat lunch
Though I'm counted on not to starve

I can't afford these breakdowns
Nor a better car

I can't afford to make money
With the money that it takes

I can't afford to mend my wallet
So the bills they all escape

I can't afford healthcare
Or the treatment I'm prescribed

I can't afford life insurance
So I better stay alive

I can't afford a lawyer
To get back what is mine

I can't afford a handgun
To commit a petty crime

I can't afford my taxes
And incur the hefty fines

I can't afford the alcohol
Which I need to unwind

I can't afford to waste time
Though good things come to those who wait

I can't afford quality
So I make another mistake

I can't afford a credit card
Because of all the fees

I can't afford the payment
To file bankruptcy

I can't afford happiness
Even though I'm told it's free

I can't afford to let you go
When you deserve more than me

# THEY WERE NEVER YOU

Casandra threw her mail down on her sleek black table, uninterested in opening all the overdue notices and "once-in-a-lifetime offers."

Casandra felt deflated as she slumped down into her overly soft couch. She reminisced how the salesman swore upon his mother's life that it would firm up after a little use. She felt gullible for believing such an obvious lie.

"She better be dead," Casandra sighed.

Staring at her dated popcorn ceiling, she wished for some excitement, or at least a reason to get up and make dinner.

Her phone chirped.

Casandra tried to pry herself out of the cushions that encompassed her completely.

Finally, she rolled to the ground, knocking a couple pillows off in the process. She checked her phone and found that a picture message from her brother, Marvin, awaited her rolling eyes.

She impatiently tapped the screen, waiting for the download progress bar to complete. She just wanted today to finish so that she could quickly get through tomorrow's boredom. Each day blended together like a stiff margarita that you never remember drinking.

The image finally came into view. It was an elderly woman looking frail and weak. "Why is he sending me this?"

Before Casandra could toss her phone back on the table, she read his note, "Mom doesn't look too great. I got this from Jacob."

*Mom?*

Casandra looked closer at the elderly woman; it was her mother. She hadn't even recognized her in such poor health.

Her thumbs frantically pounded out a response, "When was this taken? She looks like a corpse!"

Marvin wasn't writing back.

She watched the clock as a single minute went by, then five... "Hello?" she nudged, still without a reply.

Casandra needed something to take her mind off the unimaginable truth—that her mother was quite ill. She searched on the computer for assisted living places in her area and tried to budget out how she could afford such a place on a teacher's salary. She put that plan on the back burner while she put together a care package filled with comfort foods and other goodies. She forgot all about Marvin and his texts—she just kept her fingers moving. She reached for her purse to enter in her credit card number and complete her order when she noticed her phone had a blinking light on it. She had one unread message. She must have been so preoccupied that she didn't hear the notification.

It was a missed call...from Marvin, no less.

She realized how much time had slipped away. It was already 3:00 in the morning, and Marvin's call was at 2:14 a.m.

Something was wrong. She navigated her phone until she found his number, although before she could dial it, she had an incoming call. It was him.

She answered and held the device to her ear, unable to speak. On the other end, she heard his breath staggering. He was upset.

"She's gone." He barely got the words out.

Tears fell down her cheeks as she was searching for her words.

"I'll call you tomorrow, okay? I just can't right now," Marvin said softly.

"Marvin..."

"Yes?"

"I love you."

She could hear him breaking apart over the phone. He was a mess.

"I gotta go," Marvin said, followed by a click.

Casandra kept wiping her eyes with her hand, then wiping the tears on her black skirt. Her eyes were leaking like a faucet.

"Goddamn it." She picked up a pillow and buried her face inside it.

Casandra felt horrible not being able to send her care package to her mother, even though no shipping company on earth could have gotten it to her in time. She felt like a murderer from her own neglect. She wondered why she had wished for anything exciting at all. Change never comes without claiming a victim.

The next couple days were a haze. Arrangements for the service were set for the weekend, and she didn't feel up to packing. Casandra went straight to a dress store that specialized in quinceañera attire. Although Casandra wasn't Latin American, or fifteen, her petite frame allowed her to shop there, anyway.

"Give me something angry," she said to the man who greeted her at the entryway.

"Yes, ma'am," he said, stroking his mustache.

"...And make it black!" she called after him as he made his way to a rack at the far end of the store.

She got strange, teenage looks from the other customers while they tried on their ruffled gowns.

The man returned. "Sorry, ma'am. This is all I have," he held up the back of a black dress that looked...perfect, actually.

"Box it up."

The man turned the dress around revealing a huge, red rose right in the center of the bodice.

"That's the only one?" she asked, pulling on the rose, gauging how hard it would be to remove. It was really on there.

She thought about going somewhere else, but ultimately decided on the black dress with the obnoxious rose in the front.

Before leaving the mall, Casandra walked over to a coffee shop with the intention of getting a pick-me-up before her dreaded drive. She noticed, through her own reflection in the shop window, that she was a mess. Her white blouse had a fairly noticeable coffee stain on it.

*Maybe I've had enough,* she thought to herself.

Making use of the coffee shop's bathroom, she changed into the obnoxious dress that not only fit her perfectly, but also made her feel young and full of life.

The screenwriters and novelist peered up from their laptops to catch a peek. She smiled and threw her old clothes in the garbage can.

Casandra drove up the coast of California, only stopping once to see the migrating salmon in Klamath Falls. The sky changed from dark to light to dark again. Suddenly she realized she hadn't rested the whole time, though now it was too late; she was home in Newberg, Oregon. Even though it hadn't been home since her high school graduation, it still felt like it.

She pulled up to the church where the open casket was going to be a little more open than she felt comfortable with. Casandra looked down at her phone charging in the car port and realized it was only 5:04 a.m., and the service was slated for 1:00. She was much earlier than expected. She rolled up the windows of her sedan and finally got some sleep.

Casandra awoke to the sound of a hand slapping against her window. The morning sunlight had turned the car into a humid greenhouse. She lowered the windows and took in the cooler, outside air.

"Casandra, what are you doing out here?" That voice—she could never forget the high piercing wail of her aunt Doreen.

"Is it time?" Casandra asked, mid yawn.

"Almost. You can help me set up the flowers."

Casandra got out to greet her aunt with a light hug.

"You're a little moist."

"Sorry, I..."

"No, I'm the one who's sorry... She led a wonderful life. You know that, right?"

Casandra waved her hands, trying to stop the pity train. "Coffee first."

"Okay," Doreen said, fanning under her eyes.

Casandra picked up a five-gallon bucket filled with water and roses, and helped her aunt load them into the church. She paused for a moment, noticing the casket was already in place, though luckily the lid was closed.

She knew her mother was right there, though she felt so far.

"So, just put these in here," Doreen explained, as she shoved a flower inside the green florist foam that was soaking in water. Casandra remembered all the long summers working for her aunt in the flower shop. She recalled the wonderful colors and aromas, which were overshadowed by the hard work and grueling hours.

*Someone should have called child labor on her.*

The scent of fresh coffee drew her to the refreshment table, as her aunt continued to explain the ins and outs of floristry.

The industrial-sized coffee maker was struggling to spit—she knew it was almost finished.

The minister came up beside her, right as she spilled a little coffee on the church floor.

"Jesus." She was sure he was going to bust her.

"This is how you do it," the minister said, letting the coffee pour from a great height. "The oxygen makes it taste better."

*He spilled much more than I did. And only for improved taste? That has to be a sin somehow,* she thought to herself.

Casandra finished patting down both of their messes with a small square napkin.

"Should you be drinking coffee? I mean, doesn't God give you enough *divine* caffeine?"

"On the contrary, he gave me beans to roast, and hot water to percolate...and you to clean up after me."

Casandra stood up ready to fight him on faith and cross, when he handed her his oxygenated coffee.

"Try it."

She grabbed the cup out of his hand harder than she wanted to. The hot liquid swirled around the rim, almost spilling out.

She took a sip. "Mmm." She held it close to her heart. Was it better than the cup she had poured for herself? Who knew. What she did know was that at that very moment, she had faith in high-pouring coffee.

"Are there any words you want to say during the service?" the minister asked.

"No, I prefer to say goodbye in a more private way."

She started to hand the cup of coffee back to him.

"Keep it."

"Thanks, preach."

"Faith starts small, even in cynics."

"It's just coffee, geez," she mumbled to herself, making her way back to her aunt.

"You always need to cut a rose under water, like this," Doreen continued, never looking up.

Doreen reached for one of the two cups of coffee. Casandra was visibly annoyed when Doreen reached for the cup blessed by the minister.

"Did you spit in it or something?" Doreen asked, noticing her reaction.

"God, no, I just..."

"Language. This is a holy place."

"Take it." She gave up the cup.

Maybe it was all in Casandra's mind, but she winced when she tasted the cup she had poured for herself.

Casandra heard the ruckus of guests starting to arrive ahead of schedule.

*I hate it when people are early.* Her thoughts were interrupted by the sound of Jacob, her mother's longtime boyfriend and the same man who sent that scary picture the night she died.

Jacob was a devout Christian, and never approved of Casandra's sexual orientation. That explained why Marvin got the news and she didn't.

She kept her eyes on Jacob while receiving hugs from the long line of guests.

One chatty cousin pulled Casandra aside and talked all about her cat's liver problems in a hushed tone.

Before long, everyone was seated, and the casket was opened. Sitting in the front row, Casandra started to breathe shallowly. She didn't want to smell her dead mother any more than she wanted to see her. That's when she saw her brother, Marvin, for the first time in five years.

He looked great, considering his heavy eyes.

*Nothing like weddings and funerals to push you to the groomers.*

His heart-felt eulogy brought tears to everyone's eyes. Like her, he was a teacher, although he took his job very seriously, and his words showed off that fact.

Marvin was now speaking off script. He spoke about the many chicken noodle soup cans his mother made him when he was feeling ill.

"She wasn't the best of cooks, but her heart was the best of all," Marvin concluded, as another latecomer barged into the service.

Every neck got a crick that day. It was their sister, Stacy, who was late as usual. Her flowy white top contrasted perfectly with her jet-black curls.

The rest of the service was a blur. Casandra cursed her sister's tardiness. Both she and Marvin had always been punctual due to their line of work and they knew that they couldn't exactly send their sister to the principal's office.

Emotions blended with bible passages, and fond memories into warm feelings that embodied her mother's life. Tears justified her greatness. She was loved.

Casandra wished that her guests would feel like this at her own funeral.

Everyone lined up to say their last goodbyes, face to face.

Marvin stood in front of Stacy. "You didn't cry," he whispered.

"I didn't come here to."

"You obviously didn't come to hear me speak."

"I've heard enough of your lectures to last a lifetime."

"Not here." Marvin approached the casket. He touched his mother's hand and stood by her longer than everyone else had. After sharing his moment with her, he left out the back of the church.

A loud noise echoed through the room as Stacy tapped the wooden casket with one of her many rings.

*Don't look,* Casandra kept saying to herself like a broken record. She thought about fleeing the line, faking some kind of toilet emergency. It was too late. She was next. Casandra ran her fingers from one end of the casket to the other while keeping her eyes down. She heard a deflating sound and stopped cold. She knew it wasn't from her mouth, because she was holding her breath.

Casandra went against her better judgment and took a sideways glance at her mother's corpse. She thought that she looked so fake, like a wax statue. Never would her mother wear such dramatic makeup. She realized that this was not her mom, just what had been left over.

Out of habit, Casandra licked her thumb and attempted to fix her mother's smudged lipstick. She ended up smearing the foundation and uncovered the almost-gray skin underneath. She felt sick to her stomach.

Just then, the corpse blinked at her.

"Oh, God!" she belted out.

"Shhhh," the eager crowd behind her hissed like a snake.

Casandra no longer cared about her dignity. She got out of there as fast as possible.

Outside the church, everyone was bickering and fanning themselves with their programs. Nothing like black clothes on a hot day to bring the worst out in people.

Casandra made her way to her siblings who were speaking in a hushed tone.

"She looked at me," Casandra said, catching her breath.

"What?" Marvin asked.

"Mom. She blinked."

"Are you sure she wasn't just winking at you? I mean, look at what you're wearing," Stacy said.

"Hey, at least it's black and not navy. People can tell the difference, you know," Casandra said, pointing at Stacy's skirt.

"And that rose? What are you, five?"

Marvin couldn't contain his laughter any longer.

Casandra felt small again. She was the youngest, and Stacy always turned Marvin against her. It was like no time had passed.

"I'm freaking out here, and you two are back at it again," Casandra said, stomping off.

"Fine, run away like you do," Stacy yelled. "Don't get lost in all those headstones."

"Where are you going?" Marvin called out.

She realized that he was right. She had parked in front of the church.

Catching up, Marvin grabbed her by the arm. "I just needed to laugh a little. I'm sorry it was at your expense."

"Why do you let her get between us?"

"Old habits, I guess. It won't happen again, okay?" Marvin's attention was caught by the minister. It seemed that all of the guests were done with the viewing. "Come on, we have to put in her the ground now."

"I'm not going."

"Cass, you have to."

Stacy walked up next to Marvin with her arms crossed.

"I know what I saw, and I don't need to go to therapy. No offense," Casandra said, looking to Stacy. "I'll say goodbye to her in my own way, on my own terms. When is the wake?"

"It's on the invitation," Stacy snapped.

Casandra shot Jacob a foul glare, realizing she never got one. She snatched the invite from Marvin's breast pocket and quickly skimmed it. "Tomorrow? I thought everything was going to be done today? I have to get home."

"Scheduling the venue was apparently a nightmare for Doreen. Look, we'll talk tonight at Jacob's, okay?"

"Is that what we're all doing?"

"If you want an inheritance, yes," Stacy chimed in.

Casandra wrapped her arms around her brother, and he squeezed her tight. She forgot what a master of hug giving he was.

Marvin and five other pallbearers rushed back inside the church.

Casandra knew that she had to leave before that blinking zombie came outside to finish her off.

"See ya," Stacy said, turning away, not even giving Casandra the chance to show affection.

Casandra drove off to the closest grocery store and found some white carnations. She thought it would be humorous to color the flowers. It was an inside joke she shared with her mom.

*How come flowers never come in the color of cash? It would make sense because they're really just a waste of money,* she remembered her mother's words.

Casandra searched the aisles for a plastic bowl. Adding water and green food coloring, she sliced the flower stems, letting the plant soak up the dye while she continued shopping.

After an annoying amount of time, she found the finest wristwatch the store had to offer. She set the time to 9:15 and removed the battery.

The checkout lady gave her best "you gotta be kidding me" look as she set eyes upon the mess Casandra had made during her shopping adventure.

"Look, I'm paying for everything."

The checkout lady pointed at the green dye that had splashed all over the cart.

"Relax, that's what these are for," Casandra said, holding up a roll of paper towels before placing them on the conveyor belt.

The bill was just shy of a fifty, though Casandra's experience was priceless.

"Keep it," Casandra said when the checkout lady offered her the change.

"This isn't Vegas. I don't take tips," she responded, placing the coins in a box for a charity that Casandra felt very passionately against.

"No! Look what you've done," Casandra said, reaching for the jar, which had a padlock to avoid any chance of a refund being issued due to a sudden change of heart.

"It's for charity," the checkout lady scoffed.

"It's for profit," Casandra corrected as she barged out of the establishment.

Casandra found the local creek where Jeremy Meyer once broke his glasses trying to play stream slip-n-slide.

She placed the watch inside a basket while waiting for the flowers to change. She spent the remaining daylight hours relaxing. Casandra even caught a crawdad using a piece of meat that fell out of her pre-made grocery store sandwich. It wanted to snap at her with its lonely claw. As she held the adorable thing close to her face, she wanted to kiss it. She abandoned that urge after questioning the cleanliness of the mud and muck in which it lived.

Casandra hiked to her mother's favorite spot, "The Outlook." You couldn't help but admire the 360-degree view of the whole town. She placed the basket, flowers and wristwatch in place. It seemed a little sparse. She had a bright idea and grabbed the large flower on her dress and sawed at it with her keys until it came off. Placing it inside the basket really made the offering complete. She knew this was the perfect send-off for her mother, in nature.

Much to her dismay, Casandra spotted some garbage that must have blown up the hill. Upon further inspection, she saw that it was a stuffed bear, and it appeared to be new.

She looked into its black pebble eyes and noticed it had a watch imbedded in its stomach.

"What the hell?" The time was also set to 9:15. That was their time, after she had been bullied by Mike

Mercoda. Her mother declared that 9:15 was their special time, and whenever she felt sad, she was never more than twelve hours away from their moment. During those sixty seconds, nothing bad could happen to her. Casandra cherished that time twice daily until she went off to college.

Why was it up here? Was her mother trying to tell her something from beyond? Her thoughts circled around in her head like a tornado. Feeling dizzy, she decided to get out of there before the setting sun finished its routine. She could already see the moon high in the orange sky.

She drove like a drunk person, braking hard for almost-missed traffic lights and drifting out of her own lane. She made it safely to Jacob's place, or what she used to refer to as "Mom's."

Casandra burst through the door as if she had big news. In her mind, she did, although it was for select company. All the conversations abruptly ceased, leaving mouths lingering open.

"Where's Marvin?" Casandra asked the houseful of people.

An elderly man, who looked as if he couldn't remember even his own name, pointed toward the back den.

She kept her eyes to herself, hoping to avoid any distractions.

Like her previous entrance, she burst through the den's door.

"Great timing. Have a seat," Doreen said, with a guiding gesture.

The den still smelled how she remembered it, like old books. Classics lined the walls without even a single crease on their bindings. Doreen sat at the far end of an oak desk, and Cassandra's two siblings had already made themselves comfortable on the opposing side.

She meekly took the middle seat and folded her hands on her lap, feeling trapped.

"Now that you're all here, there are a bunch of things I need you to sort out. First of all, we have this box of papers and bills," Doreen started.

"Stacy can have that stuff," Marvin quipped.

She shot him a glance and reluctantly took the box, putting it under her chair.

"There are a couple boxes of pictures and personal artifacts..." Doreen continued.

"I'll take that stuff," Marvin said, ejecting himself from his seat at the opportunity.

"Now wait a second, that isn't how this works. As the executor, I have to divide everything up equally."

"I give my share of the bills and paperwork to Stacy," Marvin said.

"Me too," Casandra chimed in.

"I don't want any of that sentimental crap," Stacy admitted.

"Don't you care about anything?" Marvin snapped.

"Just the cash."

Marvin reached over Casandra and swatted his older sister.

"Will you all stop it?" Doreen yelled. "You used to get along so well when you were young."

"I don't remember that at all," Stacy said.

Doreen went searching through one of the boxes and found a picture of the three kids. Casandra looked about five years old, which would make Marvin seven and Stacy nine. They were all wide-mouthed and happy.

"Wow, look at us," Marvin said.

Stacy rolled her eyes at the image.

Casandra noticed that Stacy's hair was much lighter back then, almost blond.

"Stacy, look at the color of your hair before you dyed it," Casandra said.

"I *don't* dye my hair."

They all looked at her black locks, amazed, and exchanged disbelieving glances.

"When was this taken? I don't see a date," Marvin asked, looking at the back of the photo.

"Back at your old place. You were maybe seven or eight. Don't you recognize it?" Doreen asked.

All three of the siblings looked closely at the photograph, and uniformly shook their heads side to side.

"Nice swing, though," Casandra said, noting the large oak tree with a tire swing tied to it.

"Our house?" Marvin inquired.

"Stacy, you were nine-ish, surely you remember?" Doreen asked. "You used to insist that visitors take off their shoes when they entered."

"We always lived here, with Jacob," Stacy said.

"Well, after the incident, you did."

"The what?" Stacy asked.

"Oh, dear. Well, that brings me to the next order of business. The house..."

"I want it," Casandra blurted out.

"You can have it, if I get all the moolah," Stacy said.

"Everyone, stop! There is no money. The funeral, wake, flowers and everything else ate it all up."

*Mom was right about the flowers after all,* Casandra chuckled inside.

"Why is the wake tomorrow? Can't we just do it now and get it over and done with?" Casandra asked.

Doreen's face turned red, like a tomato. "Look, I don't want to do this anymore than you do. All her stuff is in these boxes. You guys figure it out for yourselves and let me know how you divide it up, okay? Bye," Doreen announced, storming out.

"Good job, Cass," Stacy teased.

"Enough," Marvin said.

"I know Jacob is hiding stuff. He's had access to all of mom's things since...always," Casandra said, trying to open the drawers on Doreen's side of the table.

They spent the next couple hours poring over documents, pictures and sentimental stuff that strangely held minimal significance to any of them.

"Look at this. Once upon a time, you were sporty," Casandra said, holding up a Little League trophy with Marvin's name on it.

"You can have it. It will look nice next to your team jerseys."

"This is so boring. My box is mostly old water bills," Stacy said.

"Who wants to check out this mystery house?" Casandra asked.

"What do you mean?" Marvin pried.

"I found the address in this newspaper clipping," Casandra replied.

"Why is it burnt?" Marvin asked, noticing the charred edges.

"Let's go find out."

"Fine," Stacy agreed, snatching the paper from Casandra's fingertips.

They packed all the boxes and carried them around back to avoid Jacob and the rest of the gathering.

Stacy opened up her sports car and heaps of garbage fell out of the passenger door. She shoved old drive-thru bags off the seat and onto the curb.

"You can't just litter like that," Marvin said.

Stacy shrugged, as Marvin gathered up the trash and brought it to the can.

"How am I supposed to fit all this stuff in your trunk? Are you living out of your car?" Casandra yelled from behind the hatchback.

"Shut up. I make more than both of you combined."

"You're a slob. I'm taking this stuff to my car," Casandra said.

"Cass, can I drive with you?" Marvin asked. "I don't want to get an infection."

"Follow me," Stacy said, slamming the newspaper on her dashboard. She peeled off, almost running Marvin over, and disappeared into the darkness.

Casandra started up her car and began her slow pursuit.

"How are we going to keep up?" Marvin asked.

"This is a small town, she can't go that far. Also, she can't get in without these," Casandra said, holding up some old rusty keys that she found in Jacob's desk.

They followed the far-off headlights and wheel squealing the best they could.

"Where did you find this, Cass?" Marvin asked, holding up the teddy bear with a clock-belly he found at his feet.

"That's what I rushed over here to show you to prove I wasn't going crazy."

"You were going crazy? And rushed over from where?"

She approached a stoplight, turning to stare into his blue eyes, "Mom's trying to communicate with me." She tried hard to make it sound believable.

"You mean the blinking thing? Like Morse code?"

"No, I found the bear on The Outlook. You wouldn't understand," Casandra said, looking back at the light wondering why it was taking so long.

"*I* left that bear there, for mom. We had this silly thing between us, at 9:15," Marvin said.

"Ever since Mike Mercoda?" Casandra interrupted.

"Yeah, remember how he used to pick on me?" Marvin asked.

"You're remembering it wrong. Mike Mercoda bullied me, not you."

"No, he broke my nose," Marvin said.

"He broke mine!" As she started driving again, her emotions took over and she drove more like her sister. "This isn't funny. You're scaring me."

"I took his juice box by accident, and he got really mad at me. I threw a defensive kick, and my shoe, that was two sizes too big, flew off. He grabbed it and started beating me with it," Casandra rambled on.

They squealed around a corner almost out of control. After the turn, Marvin pulled the handbrake, bringing the car to a halt. The engine groaned almost as loud as Casandra did.

"Don't do that!"

"Calm down. Think for a minute. Why would Mike Mercoda beat up a girl? Look at my nose."

Casandra was fuming, trying to get a grip on her shaking hands. "I was a tomboy. Maybe he thought I was a boy."

"Look at my face, Cass."

"I don't want to."

"Can we just drop it? Stacy is probably at the house, looting it of all its treasures," Marvin said.

"She wouldn't do that. Would she?"

"Remember that strange smell in my room? It was so bad that mom refused to tuck me in for like two months?" Marvin recounted.

"You finally found out that Stacy was hiding used kitty litter under your bed," Casandra said, with a smile.

"She was so mean to us."

"Didn't you get sick?"

"Yeah, that stunt gave me parasites."

"That's right...Marvin, Marvin, your parasites are starvin'."

"Don't quote her. It still makes me angry."

Casandra felt better knowing that they didn't share *every* memory, just the one that meant most to her.

They were circling around lost, and Stacy wasn't answering her phone.

"Maybe we should try again tomorrow," Marvin said.

"I need to go tonight."

"Why?"

"I didn't book a hotel, and I already slept in my car last night," Casandra said.

"Just stay at Jacob's, like I am."

"I would rather sleep with mom at the cemetery."

"You can't sleep in that old house. It might be filled with spiders and dust. Who knows the last time anyone did anything to it," Marvin said.

"I don't care. I just want to be alone."

"I've got an idea," Marvin said, reaching for his phone. He held it to his ear and raised his eyebrows as if he thought himself clever.

"Doreen, what is the address of the old house?" "What? No, we left over thirty minutes ago. Okay, thanks a bunch," he said, hanging up his phone. "Got it."

They were closer than they thought. A couple of twists and turns later, they found Stacy's car parked in front of a large house. Marvin and Casandra both felt quite strange setting eyes on it.

"Anything coming back?" Marvin asked.

"I feel like I've been here before, although nothing comes to mind."

"We were all here. You saw the picture," Marvin said. "Stacy should remember best. She's the oldest."

"Where is she?"

"The landscaping has really gone to hell," Marvin said, his feet breaking dirt clumps as they approached the dark, ominous porch.

Casandra's ears perked up as she heard the faint sound of a baby crying. Looking at her brother's calm demeanor, she decided not to bring up anything else that he might consider crazy. Instead, she tried to figure out which of the five or so keys on the ring fit the front door. Her shaking hands made the task nearly impossible.

"Let me do it," he demanded, taking the keyring out of her hands.

"First time's a charm," Marvin boasted, as they both heard the door lock click.

Noticing Cassandra was on edge, Marvin opened the door very slowing, making it creek loudly.

"Please stop."

He let out a chuckle and walked blindly into the dark living room.

There was a low snarling sound, like that of a rabid dog.

Suddenly, something launched out of the pitch blackness and tackled Marvin to the floor.

Marvin's shriek triggered Casandra's fight or flight instinct. She flew off the porch without looking back. The screams and rustling plagued her mind with images of Marvin's flesh getting eaten off his bones. He was a goner; she had to save herself now.

Casandra slipped, almost overshooting her car. She was frantically digging through her purse for her keys when both Marvin and Stacy came outside, laughing hysterically.

"Don't leave. Come back," Marvin called out.

"That's not funny at all. And for the record, you scream like a girl," Casandra said.

"You're the one who wanted to stay here."

Stacy turned on her flashlight and shined it directly in Casandra's face. "Have you been drinking, miss?"

Casandra put her keys back inside her purse and approached them, still looking over her shoulder, just in case. "How did you get inside?"

"I found a broken window."

"Was it broken before you found it?" Casandra asked.

Stacy shrugged.

"Anything interesting inside?" Marvin butted in.

"Only...I call master bedroom!" Stacy said, running back inside the house with a child-like spring in her step.

"She always does this. I should have seen it coming," Marvin said.

As far as they could tell, the house had little to no furniture in it, just open space.

"We need power," Casandra said, pulling out her phone.

"I already called them. It should be on sometime between now and tomorrow," Stacy said.

"That's typical. What about the water?"

Stacy walked into the kitchen, leaving Marvin and Casandra alone in the dark. She turned the sink faucet and a loud groaning sound came from the pipes. All throughout the house, the walls rumbled. A violent rush of water mixed with air jerked out of the faucet. A strong smell of sulfur filled the room as the cloudy water rushed out.

"I know why there were so many water bills," Stacy called out, realizing that no one ever turned it off.

"Gross, Stacy. Light a match next time," Casandra said, walking into the kitchen.

"First one who smelt it, dealt it," Marvin interjected, covering his nose, steps behind her.

Stacy pulled out a lighter from her pocket.

"Don't! I was joking. Burning sulfur will create sulfur dioxide, which could suffocate us," Casandra said, putting her years of teaching chemistry to good use.

"I bet you wish I had flatulence now," Stacy said.

"You can die from lighting your farts, too, you know. I had a student once..." Marvin said.

"Marvin," Stacy warned, holding her palm frontwards like a stop sign.

Casandra couldn't stop giggling. "I have to admit, it is the funniest way to go."

"He got seriously hurt, Cass. It's not funny," Marvin said.

"It's a *gas*," Casandra quipped.

"Let's just change the subject, please," Stacy said, leaving the room.

Casandra and Marvin followed her like little ducklings, since she had the only light source.

As they investigated the house, each room left more questions than it answered. Every mirror they found was cracked beyond repair. There were small articles scattered everywhere; it wasn't exactly empty, though it didn't appear to be lived in. Marvin found a rusty shovel and used it like a walking stick to maneuver around, gaining his independence from Stacy's light.

They followed some deep grooves or scratch marks which drew a line from the backyard, through the kitchen, to a stairwell leading down.

"It's time," Stacy said, holding the flashlight to her chin, making her face glow ghoulishly. "The basement awaits."

The thought of entering the basement of this eerie house made a chill run down Casandra's spine.

"What if whatever made those marks lives down there? What if it's hungry?" Casandra tried to convince them against the idea.

Each step creaked as Stacy slowly put one foot in front of another. She held the light to her face again as she narrated. "Little did Cass and Marvey know that these were the last steps they were ever going to make, as they inched closer to their own doom." Stacy lost her grip, the light tumbled down the stairs and turned off.

The air felt thick and old as it wafted out of the depths.

"This seems much steeper than any basement I've ever been in," Stacy said.

"Stop trying to scare us," Casandra said.

"I'm just giving you facts. It's not my fault if you're scared of the truth."

They finally reached solid ground, blindly crawling around on their hands and knees, looking for the light.

"Oh, Jesus!" Casandra blurted out as she touched something fleshy and warm.

"It's just me," Marvin said.

"Oh, hey," Stacy said clicking away on her lighter.

"Give it here, you were never good at child locks," Marvin said.

"Catch," Stacy said, tossing the lighter towards his voice. It bounced and exploded upon hitting a stone wall.

"How was that a good idea, Stacy?" Marvin asked.

"Shh, I found something," Casandra said.

"The light?" Stacy asked.

"I don't think so."

"Keep talking; I'm coming to you," Marvin said, scrambling around.

Casandra whistled a tune like a song bird, leading him to her.

"What song is that?" Marvin asked.

"I dunno, it's just in my head."

"I feel it...it has like a hinge, I think. I'm opening it," Marvin said.

"Don't."

"Some fabric...and...bones," Marvin said.

Casandra screamed like she was on a roller coaster for the first time.

"This wasn't the best idea, guys," Stacy admitted.

A huge flash of light blinded all three of them.

"What the heck was that," Stacy said.

The light went away just as fast as it had come.

"Aliens?" Casandra suggested.

"That hurt," Marvin said, covering his eyes with his hand.

Again, the light came, only this time it stayed on.

Dark spots blurred their vision as the scene came into focus.

"Good old power company, always unpredictable," Stacy said.

The basement was an oddly shaped room. The floor was solid earth. In the center stood an ornate wooden box with the top opened.

"That looks like a coffin to me," Casandra said.

"It's too small," Stacy pointed out.

"It's a box, with bones in it—that's the exact definition of a coffin," Marvin countered.

"Good point," Stacy said, walking over to the box. She looked down upon it with a scrunched-up nose. "It's animal remains. Look at how small the femur is."

"I'll take your word for it," Casandra said.

"This is why I always flushed my pets down the toilet," Stacy said, proudly.

"Can we get out of here? It's really freaking me out," Casandra asked.

"Oh, hey, my flashlight," Stacy said, picking up the thing.

Casandra swiped the light out of her hands and used it to illuminate her path upstairs while her siblings debated the source of the bones.

Upon reaching the top of the stairs, Casandra felt like something was terribly off. She realized that the house was immaculate. No spider webs, dust or signs of the place being abandoned.

*Who has been here?*

The house lights flickered as she had the thought.

*If you can hear me, stop it.*

She waited for a response, then realized that she didn't really think that one through as the light stayed consistent.

"With the right coat of paint, we could get a fair amount for this place." Casandra heard her siblings talking as they walked up the stairs.

"Shhh, did you guys see that?"

"See what?" Stacy asked.

"The light flickered."

"It was fine down here," Marvin said.

Casandra started to get that deja vu feeling.

"I fell..." Casandra started to search for the spot. "...over there!" She ran into the kitchen and felt around with her hand. "Light, light." She snapped her fingers for the flashlight she had left near the stairs. Most of the kitchen bulbs were burned out.

Marvin handed her the flashlight, and she pointed it at a gouge in the wooden floor.

"I banged my tooth there. I think I'm starting to remember this place," Casandra admitted.

"You're crazy," Stacy said.

"I'm starting to remember stuff too. Wasn't there a piano in the living room?" Marvin added.

"Not you, too."

Casandra and Marvin both ran over to a spot near a huge window. The shape of a piano had protected the floor's finish from the sun's rays.

"It was right here. I knew it!" Marvin said.

"Stacy, you are old, what do you remember?" Casandra asked.

"Nothing. Honestly, this house feels as cold as a hospital."

"Just try," Marvin pressed, pretending to sit at the old the piano bench.

Marvin and Casandra both started to hum a tune in unison. It was haunting how they both started on the same key at the same tempo.

A gust of wind blew open a window shutter; it rattled against the wall in rhythm with their duet.

Stacy started backing away toward the door, her mouth agape. "How did you guys do that?"

Marvin approached her, reciting forgotten lyrics while waltzing with an imaginary partner.

"I'm out," Stacy said, reaching for the front door.

"Don't go," Casandra said, breaking the melody.

"I don't think I've ever heard that song before, but I know it somehow," Marvin said.

"I feel the same way. Stacy?"

"Why would I know that song? It sounds very old-fashioned."

"I remember this house. We really did live here," Casandra said.

"I know, right?" Marvin agreed.

"Are you guys getting back at me for ditching you, because you look certifiable—like one of my patients," Stacy said.

"How so?" they both said in unison.

"It's in your eyes. Both of you. It's like you're not seeing what is in front of you, but beyond. Like you're seeing something else in your mind," Stacy said, popping a pill out of a prescription bottle.

"You really don't remember this house?" Marvin asked.

"Just stay your distance for a minute."

"I'm not trying to pressure you. I just find all of this really fascinating," he conceded.

Stacy bit on her lower lip and shook her head slowly back and forth.

"Let's give her some space. We need supplies, anyway," Marvin told Casandra.

"I'll be in my room," Stacy said, heading up the circular staircase.

They drove to the local liquor store which was a block away from their old elementary school.

"I remember this store. Mom used to give me five dollars for lunch. I would buy the cheapest snack I could find and use the rest at that comic book store that used to be next door," Marvin said, looking at the laundromat where it used to reside.

"I did the same thing. Chilly dog, and a fruit drink—that was the cheapest."

"How could that be? The comic book store closed before you went to elementary school," Marvin said.

"Don't start with that again."

"You could have remembered going there with me."

"No, *I* remember going there."

"Then you're remembering it wrong."

"Don't tell me what I do and do not remember!"

"Here, get the supplies, and I will call Doreen to get a second opinion," Marvin said.

Casandra went into the store, flustered. First, he remembered her memory, now he claimed that she was remembering his. She quickly grabbed light bulbs, water, snacks, a space blanket, a hand mirror and astronaut freeze-dried ice cream for Marvin.

Casandra made her payment, and the store clerk offered out a fistful of change. Casandra weighed her options. The clerk was within reach of another charity box she didn't approve of. She reluctantly received her change with a disgusted look on her face. On her way out of the store, Casandra tossed her receipt and the coins into the garbage.

"That doesn't go in there," a voice scoffed at her.

"Oops," she tried to play it off as a mistake. Turning to find that it was only a homeless man, she knew he had no means of getting her in trouble.

"That's a federal offense."

"So is loitering."

"You obviously don't care about our forefathers and what they went through for our freedom."

"You're all about the word 'free,' aren't you?"

"I'm not the terrorist who's throwing away American currency."

"I wasn't throwing it away, I was leaving this for you. Isn't that where you do your shopping?" Casandra pointed at the garbage can.

The homeless man started to pull back his dirt-stained sleeves and Casandra knew he wasn't above punching a woman, or probably a baby, for that matter.

She decided to disengage and hurry to her car. Casandra got into the driver's seat, quickly locking the door. Marvin was deep in conversation. He raised his finger to her.

She drove back to the mysterious house, trying to make sense of Marvin's incessant "uh-huhs."

About the time she parked, he got off the phone.

"What did she say?"

"Jacob wants those boxes back. Apparently, we took the wrong ones."

"No, I mean about the comic book store."

"Oh, she said she was never a fan of comics. Let's check out the backyard," Marvin said.

They made their way around the side of the house, looking for anything that seemed out of the place.

"This is quite a big yard, but where are all the trees? Didn't the picture have trees?" Marvin asked, shining the flashlight around.

"Look at the edge of the lot," Casandra said.

All the neighboring trees were bent in a peculiar way, away from the property.

"That's weird...also, not a single blade of grass," Marvin added.

Casandra noticed a flash of light dart through the darkness. "What was that?"

The flashlight started to flicker, and Marvin started banging on its side.

"It's running out of juice. Did you buy batteries?" Marvin asked.

"I knew I forgot something." Casandra got up the courage to approach where the light had come from, thinking it might be her mother guiding her. She found something sticking out of the earth in the very same spot. "Get me the shovel," she demanded, digging at the hard dirt with her bare hands.

"Uh, okay. Just a minute." He placed the light on the ground, pointed at her.

The moment he left, a sound flowed through the breeze. It was almost like words. She tried to make it out; it was on the tip of her tongue.

"Ten, nine, eight, seven..." the words finally came to her. She covered her ears to make them stop.

"Here," Marvin thrust the shovel at her, scaring her half to death.

"We need to get you a bell," Casandra pushed it back at him.

"Like a cat?"

"Exactly. I never know when you're coming or going."

Marvin started digging in the ground where Casandra directed. There was definitely something buried.

They unearthed a large, colorfully striped box, and dragged it inside the house, leaving a trail of dirt.

"Stacy!" Casandra yelled.

"Get down here!" Marvin added.

They heard the sound of a car quickly peeling away. They rushed to the window, but she was already gone.

"She *was* really spooked," Marvin said.

"No, she just drives like that." Casandra unwrapped the plethora of bulbs she had purchased and started to brighten up the place. "Should we go after her?"

"No, I'll call her," Marvin said, pulling out his phone.

Let's look in this buried treasure first. We don't want her calling dibs again."

"All right."

They opened the sealed box, and dust blew into their eager faces.

"I hope it's not anthrax," Casandra said, coughing.

Inside, they found a bunch of different medical folders. They each grabbed a stack and flipped through them.

"Funny, no last names," Marvin pointed out.

"Also, they're all women," Casandra said, holding an X ray to the light as if she knew how to read it.

"They look really outdated."

"I know what these are..." Marvin said, the color vanishing from his face.

Casandra snatched the file from his hand, thinking it held the answer.

"I don't get it. What is it?" Casandra asked, tossing the file in the pile.

"Abortions."

"What? No."

"Look. There are dates." He pointed at a page inside one of the files. "That was way before the laws changed. It was illegal back then."

"You're right, all of these women were pregnant."

"Maybe the person who built this house was a doctor and hid his evidence in the backyard to elude conviction."

"That means those bones..." Casandra said, not wanting to finish her sentence.

"...were human. And I touched them," Marvin said, running to the sink to wash his hands.

"I didn't buy soap, sorry."

"Call Stacy. Ask her to bring some."

Casandra picked up her phone and called her sister. They heard her phone ringing from upstairs.

"She must have left it," Casandra yelled.

Marvin came into the room focused on the sound. They followed it up the stairs to the top floor.

"It's coming from here," Marvin said, as he followed the ring tone.

They opened the double doors leading into the huge master bedroom.

They found her phone on an antique side table, along with her purse.

"Don't do that," Marvin said, as he watched his sister rifle through it.

"She left her keys..." Casandra continued to pilfer through the leather purse.

"What?"

"Let's see what pills you're stealing, Stacy." She pulled out the prescription bottle.

"I'm sure it's a painkiller."

"It was prescribed. It's got her name on it."

"Give it here."

"What is Risperidone? I bet it's an appetite suppressant. That's why she's so skinny. Busted."

"Hold on, I'm looking it up."

She

took out a pill and put it in her palm, "Let's live in Stacy's world," Casandra said, popping the medication into her mouth."

"Spit that out. It's an antipsychotic medication."

"Too late..." Casandra said, opening her mouth wide, proving that she had swallowed it. "But let's be honest, we always knew she was crazy."

"You *never* take another person's pills, and you *never* use someone else's hairbrush."

"That was a long time ago, Marvin, and you still can't prove anything."

"I had evidence. Your dirty, little hairs were stuck in all the bristles."

"Fine, I used it. And after you caught me, I used it more. I just removed my hair from it afterwards. Is that what you want to hear?"

Marvin gagged. "Now that we're being honest with each other, I made out with your ex."

"Bree? You crossed your heart and hoped to die." Casandra chased him out of the room.

"You will stick no needles in these blue eyes," Marvin yelled behind him.

The house was big and elaborate; their playful tones echoed throughout the hallways.

Casandra got images of playing a game with her imaginary friend—herself. Although she was different somehow.

"I'm getting something..."

"Time out," Marvin said, resting his hands on his knees as he caught his breath.

"Hide-and-go seek. I was 'it,' and I found you in the..."

"...breakfast nook. Except I was the one who found you," Marvin said.

Casandra shook off his comment, not wanting to lose the memory. "Stacy was hiding somewhere new...but where?"

"Do you feel that?" Marvin asked.

Casandra slowly nodded her head, a tingling feeling coming over her entire body.

"Marvin...uh...your hair is sticking up."

"Yours is, too."

Casandra ran to the grocery bags and pulled out the hand mirror. Sure enough, her hair was frizzy and almost floating. Behind her she saw a dancing light on the floor.

"Marvin!"

"What is it?"

"Look in the mirror," she said, handing it to him.

His face confirmed that she wasn't going crazy this time.

"It's gone now," Casandra said, looking at the spot behind them.

"No, look," Marvin said. Sure as day, it was still dancing around inside the reflection. It went over to the spot where the piano had been and swayed back and forth. It almost looked like a human shadow, only it was made of light instead of darkness.

"I think it's mom," Casandra whispered.

The light darted around the floor, until it finally went downstairs.

"The basement," they both said to each other and ran down the stairs, skipping every other step.

"I don't get it. There's nothing down here, just dirt," Casandra said.

"No light shadow, either."

Casandra was happy Marvin had seen it too; she thought the pill might have been making her crazy.

Marvin kept pacing around, ducking his head under the floodlamp above as he passed by it.

"Doesn't this room seem a little strange, like shorter?" Marvin thought aloud.

"The dirt floor."

"Let's dig."

They ran upstairs and got the shovel. Pushing aside the wooden box, they took turns piling the dirt on either side of the room.

As they dug, they recounted their earliest memories. Pushing down their emotions and analyzing their findings objectively, they concluded that every memory, during the time they lived in the house, they both shared, and every memory after they moved to Jacob's gave them each a different perspective. The more they talked it over, the more they remembered.

Hours went by until the piles met the ceiling. Suddenly, they hit something solid. They both used their hands to uncover a trapdoor. Marvin tried the knob, but it was locked.

"The keys," Casandra exclaimed.

They both rushed upstairs.

"What do you think you're doing?" they heard a voice that wasn't either of theirs.

They both screamed loudly, and soon realized it was Stacy.

"You're back. Good," Marvin said.

"I never left. Why did you go through my things?" Stacy asked, holding up her purse.

"We saw your car leave. Don't lie," Casandra said.

"No...Jacob stole my car. I ran after him, but I was too late."

"Why would Jacob do such a thing?" Marvin contested.

"He came by saying he needed the boxes back. It seemed weird, so I lied and told him they were in my car and I had to get the keys. When I went upstairs to call you, I heard the engine start and ran after him."

"He wanted something in one of the boxes," Marvin said.

"Let's find out what it is," Casandra said, knowing they were in her car.

"I already took the liberty. You really should lock your doors, Casandra," Stacy said, waving an envelope.

Marvin reached for it and Stacy pulled it away. "First, what are you two doing?"

"I think we found a secret room under the basement," Casandra said.

Stacy relinquished the note to her brother's eager hands.

He tore it open like a child on Christmas and read it aloud, "Kids, I've spent too long hiding this secret. I often tried to bring us all together, but something always got in the way. Ending my life was the only way I could guarantee you all would be together on this anniversary. Insanity doesn't run in our family, it never has. Trust the signs. Make it right again. I love you so much, Mom." Marvin looked up. "It has today's date."

"She killed herself?" Casandra hid her sorrow in her hands.

"I don't understand," Marvin added, also tearing up.

"Maybe the answers are in that room," Stacy suggested.

Cassandra grabbed the keys and the flashlight. Marvin wiped his face on his shoulder, and they all went downstairs together. Sure enough, one of the old keys unlocked the door.

The door was so small that they had to enter one at a time. Climbing down the ladder, they found a large room with an old, metal operating table in the center. Archaic surgical instruments were neatly placed on a TV tray.

It felt like they had stumbled into a time capsule. The room was fully dressed from decades past.

The floor had a message painted on it, "Forgive me. I will give back what has been taken."

Casandra tried to keep her cool and pointed the flashlight at the other side of the room. That side seemed almost void of light. She slowly walked toward the corner. The flashlight flickered.

"What is it?" Stacy asked.

"Stop!" Marvin yelled.

Casandra almost stumbled into a square pit, its walls and floor painted black. Tubes and other mechanisms pointed at the pit from above. She followed them with the flashlight until she reached the far wall.

"What's that?" Stacy asked.

The light revealed a wall filled from floor to ceiling with human fetuses in jars.

"I'm going to be sick," Marvin blurted out.

The tubes were connected to enormous glass flasks filled with red liquid.

The effects of the medication started to kick in and Casandra felt strange, as she started to remember everything. She staggered over to her siblings like a drunk person.

"What's wrong with her?" Stacy asked.

"She took one of your pills."

"Why would anyone do that? Do you know what they're for?"

"Schizophrenia," Marvin said.

"We were playing hide-and-seek. Stacy hid down here in the secret room," Cassandra began.

"No, I didn't."

"It took use forever, but we found the door. She was crying."

"It's the pills, they're making her hallucinate," Stacy reasoned.

"She fell inside the pit. We tried to pull her out, but we also fell in."

Stacy pulled out a pistol and pointed it directly at Casandra. "I told you to stop!"

"Stacy, where did you get that?" Marvin gasped.

"It's mine. She got it from my car," Casandra slurred.

"Just put the gun away. We all need to calm down," Marvin pleaded.

"I told you to just let it go, but you kept on prying," Stacy warned.

"You know something, Stacy," Marvin said.

"No, I don't. None of this makes any sense. You guys are acting crazy, and I have to put a stop to it."

"But you *are* hiding something," Casandra stated.

Marvin stumbled backwards over a newspaper. It had the same picture of the house that they all saw at Jacob's, only this one wasn't burned. Marvin read the headline out loud, "Intruder murders local man. Mr.

Haldwin was found stabbed nineteen times with a kitchen knife."

"I didn't mean to. The voices were telling me to. He was going to take my body away from me. I'm better now. The pills turn off the voices."

"That's what mom was covering up," Marvin said.

"Stacy, put down the gun," Casandra ordered.

"What do you mean, bury the secret?" Stacy said to herself.

"Marvin, the bottle said every four hours. It's been longer than that," Casandra whispered. *Please don't let me die like this.*

A huge gust of wind came down the trapdoor and knocked Stacy over. The gun went off.

Casandra's stomach hurt. She grabbed the gun with a bloody hand. "Get in the pit," she demanded, turning the gun on Stacy.

"We never asked for this," Stacy pleaded.

"Cass, what are you doing?" Marvin said.

"Now!"

Stacy crawled into the pit, complying with her wishes. "Please don't hurt me."

"Father flipped the switch thinking it was for the light. Instead, it turned on all of this. The crazy doctor's experiment worked. I remember floating high above my crying body, wondering why I was so sad. Something was fighting me for control. I had lost, and that is when she protected me. She bore the burden for us both," Casandra said. "It was then that we all switched bodies. You for me and me for you." She looked at Marvin.

"And Stacy?"

"For something else."

"Don't flip that switch. You don't know what it will do. It might kill her, or worse. She's our sister. I really think the pills are messing with you right now," Marvin begged.

"She's already dead." Casandra pulled the large switch. Electricity flowed through the red liquid and through the fetus jars. Black mist blew into the pit, and Stacy screamed.

An electric surge caused the jars to burst, spilling their contents on the floor.

Stacy's screams faded, and Casandra turned off the device.

Casandra hobbled to the smoking pit.

Marvin couldn't bear to remove his hands from his face. He hoped that he hadn't just witnessed a murder.

Casandra looked down and saw Stacy. She had much lighter hair, like in the photograph. She was alive. "Stacy, are you okay?"

Stacy turned her innocent eyes to Cassandra, "I don't like this game. I've been hiding here for a very long time," her childlike voice rang out.

"It's okay now," Cassandra said, reaching down to her sister. "All the voices in your head, they were never you."

The End

# BE CALM

I'm always quick to indulge in my desires

Be calm, be calm

It's far past my own control
Like an addict, I need help
Asking for what you need is admitting there is a problem

I don't have a flaw
I am it

Be calm

I used to surround myself with things I love
Now I sell them, piece by piece

My riches are being plundered
Like a miner hollowing out my veins
They were part of me
But now you're all of me

I need a plan for myself for when I am completely empty

What will be left to love

Be calm

I cannot buy back my memories
Nor can I live in the behind
Looking forward into the face of the fast-approaching train

As far as the world is concerned, I am nothing
I have nothing to lose in proving it wrong

Calm yourself, and just be

# THE OTHER SIDE OF BORROWED TIME

I cannot be bothered to turn on the lights—it will only illuminate all the unwashed dishes, dirty laundry and garbage that are invading my apartment.

Inside the darkness of my desire, a vacuum produces a chill out of nothing. Trading cold for pain in a mutual exchange. I'm starved for happiness within the famine built for myself. In the afterhours of my mind, I must return the hurt for a full refund.

I feel like a stone, too depressed to move, yet too hardened to do anything about it.

Never a caller calling, nor a friend popping in. Only solicitations paid—buying a conversing moment from a whorish mouth. The junk piles up upon a tower of defeat.

Tonight seems longer than usual. Maybe the sun took a holiday, or gave up completely—something I could never do. I've tried before, and only in my failure did I find a new low, even for myself.

No one misses me when I'm here, why would they when I'm gone?

My iron-clad stomach can digest any pills, in any amount. Once I tried to punish it by giving up on eating altogether. I soon found that I'm a slave to its sensation and ended up eating even more than before. My extra pounds are another sign of my defeat.

Empty dreams next to empty bottles. Weak rope next to a strong appetite. I hide myself deep inside the rich flavors. The artificial feeling to help me forget—only my esteem remembers the numbness.

So, I wait for nothing and feel surprised it comes in abundance.

Cold hands have nothing heartfelt to write, nothing worth a read, nothing to put to the page—only blank as my walls, white and drab—no name to address the smell seeker of the future's find.

After attempting to write on a greasy burger wrapper, I realize how silly my life has become.

Nothing can hurt me more than myself. Dull blades ignore my sharp senses while I reform a plan.

In an endless supply of butter knives and yarn, I'm left with no viable options. I need to restock with weapons of mass execution. So, I leave my small tomb of an apartment.

In the dead of night, in the dead of my heart, the bricks pile as high as my hopes used to bleed. In my distant memory, from a time when anything was possible, I was a propitious wreck. This was before I learned the truth, that I was exempt from a happy ending. Though now I'm seeking all I can grasp, which is half of the story—the part you leave on the cutting room floor, if only you sharpened your sword properly.

I walk through the worst part of town, looking everyone directly into their evil eyes. I'm looking for a fight, one that I will gladly take a dive in—not for money or fame but for an end. Bullies want to victimize, not satisfy an emotionally dying person. Flashing wads of cash makes them avoid me even further, as if I were part of some sting operation.

To euthanize is to be virtuous—a trait hidden from the blackest of hearts, where no pleasure is gained from fulfilling a wish.

The bright florescent lights of the corner store pierce my eyes with their artificial shine as I enter. The door doesn't "bing" at the sight of me, like it usually does. I almost miss its introduction.

Even now, faded from the world, a premonition of things to follow, a haunting gasp escapes my hollow shell.

I walk right past the rat poison, giving it slight pause. No one wants to die a rodent's death. I move on to a much cleaner method, finding the cleaning supplies. I will unclog my wicked insides with a bottle of drain cleaner. It is a failsafe method, one that cannot be reversed.

I hold the hungry poison which yearns for an introduction to my interior. This is the last attempt at failure, my last attempt at giving up.

I feel self-conscious about this lonely buy and contemplate adding other filler, to not let on to my ultimate plan. After picking up a pack of twelve sponges another thought forms.

Suspicion comes from care, a package that is never addressed to you.

I return the diversion back to its place and hear a sound of delight and playfulness. I turn my head to spot a couple, cuddling and loving, despite being in a place like this. They couldn't show restraint even if they wanted to, and I know they don't want to.

Then I see her, envy. Arms tightly wrapped around a life I never had the opportunity to have. She was grown from an angel's garden, while I rot on the butcher's floor.

Everything is fun and free as they laugh at the simplest of things, an ingredient or a design on a package. She hugs him as he tickles her neck with his adoring nose, taking in her scent, making her part of him, inside.

They're glowing all around, like two perfect bulbs of jealousy, burning everything they touch, and it touches me, deeply.

Kind and courteous, they both apologize and thank a stranger whom they blocked from the aisle while entranced inside their public display.

She is far nicer than I could ever be—polite and genuine, nearly unreal—like a movie sprouted to life, a flash of fiction manifesting before me. No wonder he loves her. I see it in his smile, in his touch. He is radiating a sensation I never knew. Maybe if I had a chance to indulge in the other side, I might find my muscles and resist the urge of endlessness.

Their arms reach out until fingertips alone are left touching as they say farewell for only a brief moment. She needs privacy in acquiring her next item of purchase. As a woman, I understand her modesty. I can tell he misses her already, as the glow fades.

Her bubbly head disappears out of sight, leaving him alone, unsuspecting. My vampire-like thirst is out for blood. Nothing left to lose, when nothing is left to live.

I empty my arms of the caustic jug and stalk his back from behind, as his shadow.

Like a found treasure in the turbulent sea, I reach around him as she once did, before she abandoned the spot still warm from the closeness they shared.

My imposterous embrace brings the glow back to his being. He falls for it—he falls for me. I experience how lucky she is, how much life their love gives. Tears of happiness fill my deceitful eyes as a smile emerges out of my dark cave of a mouth.

I feed on what I crave, fitting perfectly inside her dainty shoes. The light touches me in a way that hope is made. It is a misplaced emotion I took without asking from an uncharted map.

I steal her love as he caresses my lonely, false arm. I feel the darkness cleansing from inside me, dissipating out of my breath like invisible mist. I lust for his adoration. He gives me real sensation, not artificially, and I mirror back the emotion. If only I could be her forever.

I have found what I've been looking for, if only for a moment. It can never last, it never has to. The only problem is, I'm now addicted to prismatic feelings, bright and beautiful.

I hear her cheerful stride as she skips back to the man. The very one who, unknowingly, has no vacancy. Before getting caught, I release my hold from his tender body and slip away.

Slithering back from whence I came, I resurrect a vow into a new life of fuzzy feelings, awoken from the long winter that was nearly eternal.

I will dedicate my life to finding that feeling again. Only this time it will be earned, and real, and mine.

The End

# IN THE NAME OF THE CHUMP

the first lie
call it a party

no one has fun
inside this debauchery

bite and claw
tearing limb from limb

two dead-headed corpses
spiting venom

they feed on each other
hating the taste

it grows from inside
until making waste

poisoning blood
and coming out

like the endless foam
from a rabid mouth

doomed to suffer
too lazy to stand

was it some hidden file
or a grabby hand

become what you hate
from what you ate
in a vicious cycle
we all helped create

~~¡FUCK TRUMP!~~

# HEAVEN CAN WEIGHT

Gluttony has always been the warden of heaven's "waistline dress code." Not only is being obese a sin, it is the biggest, fattest one.

It's a, somewhat, unspeakable law that has been passed down from Adam and Eve and their nudist lifestyle. Back in those days, keeping a keen physique was an act of restraint, willpower. Trading faith for famine, feast for figure—these are the ways to be underindulgent and overzealous.

Why else do most old people get quite skinny before checking into the afterlife? They eat like a bird, so they can fly like one. It's similar to packing a bag, or checking the local weather before taking a big trip. Old people are acting on the unspoken law about being heavy in heaven, because they *are* taking the longest trip of all...to the very place they bought—the farm.

When I was younger, I used to believe that Saint Peter had a scale where he would weigh you in, and that each sin you had committed in life made you a little heavier. Maybe this was all inspired by my mother telling me to "Eat soft and pray hard."

Once, I asked a minister at a wedding reception, "What if a really overweight person is able to get past Peter's scale, and gets in?" He looked at me like I was crazy, or genned in on some religious secret. In either case, what he told me, I remember to this day. He said that the clouds in heaven are very light, and if someone weights too much, they will fall back down to earth. I thought that I had just acquired the path to endless life through reincarnation.

Ever since that day, I've been doing my part to end the world's hunger that continues inside the round globe I call my stomach.

I've been called a heathen for not wanting to spend the rest of my days on an everlasting diet. Cleanliness is next to godliness when I'm cleaning up a deep-fried, bacon, jalapeno pizza.

I've never seen anything wrong with having a few extra pounds for 'dem mounds. Which begs the question, "Is the afterlife really worth sacrificing the one life you have here on earth for?" Some say "yes," others say "no," but I ask a question to that question, "Is there cake in heaven?" It may sound silly, or a little superficial, but cake represents an idea of happiness—past, present and future. Almost everyone has been conditioned to think this way. It doesn't matter if you're gluten-free, sugar-free or, like in my case, ice cream cake makes you throw up...you eat whatever cake it is and blissfully enjoy every minute of it—even when it comes up a second time.

I believe cake is the human flaw, something we cannot resist even when we want to. Eating cake is the very moment we lose ourselves completely and throw all of our core beliefs out the window. It's God's "back-door" into our programing—to make us do things we're not proud of. Like that time I ate a whole cake before my wife's birthday party and had to buy a second one before she got home. Am I proud of that? No. Am I happy I did it? You bet your ass.

Every time we're in a restaurant and the staff stars to sing their horrendous version of the beloved Happy Birthday song (to avoid copyright issues), we sing and clap along in the hopes that they will offer us a slice.

Birthdays are the only holiday where it's mandatory to eat cake. You have to eat that cake, and eat it good, until you're so full that you actually feel pregnant, yourself. Some may even think it to be a sinister tradition—singing a monotone song, while presenting a gluttonous, fiery offering. It could be the devil's doing; so good it's bad, so bad it's good.

The first two birthdays didn't have cake, and we all know how well they turned out. No one would have given two shits about that apple if cake had been around.

Since then, God realized (in his infinite wisdom) that babies and cake are two of the most beautiful things this world has to offer, and incorporated them into a single day.

If cake *was* offered in heaven, the world on earth would be a totally different place, indeed. People might stop eating altogether, just to get there faster. Overcrowding would ensue, heaven would soon be at maximum occupancy, and the fire department would shut them down. The whole world would be in disrepair and unrest.

There are many similarities between the "place after death" and the "thing you would die for." First, they both have a fluffy center. Second, there is always a line to get to them both. Lastly, even if you live a boring, worthless life, heaven is known as the "icing on the cake."

So, my question no longer seems asinine at all, does it? Life and death are two sides of the same story, and celebrating one without the other seems like blasphemy, if I do say so myself.

Right or wrong, heaven or hell, fat or thin, right now, I can guarantee one finite truth; all you can think about is cake!

The End

## HE STARES AT ME

Today I slaughtered my other self in the mirror. I felt his pain as my own.

One of us was laughing, while the other was crying.

Stealing the light that enriched his eager eyes left me alone in darkness.

I don't know which side of the glass I was on.

lb blinks. If not, slowly press an
ENTER button until the light bul
after the light bulb blinks press
complete the pro[illegible]mming.

*existing Ke[illegible]Entry*

grammed PIN [illegible] want
d the # button until the light

4-digit PIN of your choice,
tton. The light bulb will blin

# THE LONELY POISON

Most people go out to dinner as a means of being somewhat social—either by meeting up with someone they have already made the acquaintance of, or in the hopes of meeting someone new. No one *wants* to eat alone. I take that back—no one wants to be *seen* eating alone.

I take solace in my store-bought frozen delicacies. Yes, they ignore all nutritional guidelines and are most possibly aiding and abetting in my lonesomeness—pushing me further into a calorie-enriched depression.

Grocery stores sell these pathetic "meals for one" to further drive in the point that we're so very alone. Some of those "heat and serve" meals are quite good actually, assuming your standards for yourself and your life have hit rock bottom. It's almost as embarrassing as buying condoms or tampons, except in those cases, you have someone waiting for you at the end of your journey.

I once saw a family of four buying multiple single-person packages. It was the first time I scoured the aisle holding my head up high. I mean, if a family could buy these meals, then who's to say that I too don't have a couple of littles waiting for me at home? My comfort quickly dissolved when a small girl approached me with an inquisitive look about her. I knelt down, hoping to help her with whatever was troubling her, maybe pass off some words of wisdom to the pig-tailed kid. Instead, she invited me to eat dinner at her home. Before I even had a chance to reject her preposterous offer, her mother pulled her in with a nervous arm and stated, "No, honey, there has to be a reason why a man his age doesn't have a family of his own to eat with."

As much as it hurt, there was some truth to her words. When you have nothing in your life giving you happiness, you must lower your standards with a depressant—making even normal life seem exceptional.

I spent the rest of the night talking to the bottom of a sherry bottle. I know what you're thinking, "Who drinks sherry?" Well, the answer to that is, "Alcoholics do." When you drink as much as I do, you run out of everything, and in a desperate moment you have to chug the bottom of the barrel. In my case, it's the sherry I bought for making eggnog a couple years back. Yes, it was old, but I *was* getting drunk off the stuff. And no, it didn't taste better with age.

Life eventually forces you to change your ways and break the cycle, even if you dread the results. I was out of liquid poison, and never ended up buying my "meal for one" due to the aforementioned humiliation. What I should have done was resupplied my liquor cabinet. I don't even know why I have the empty piece of furniture. Yet another useless part of my life, wasting space.

Out of options, I put on my bomber jacket over my tank top and staggered to the closest bistro that also served liquor. I was more interested in the booze, but I knew I needed to have something solid inside me to throw up later.

Normally, I would have sat outside on the patio, but it was much colder than normal. Even my bomber jacket wasn't warm enough on this particular night.

When I asked about turning on the patio heaters, the host looked at me like I was crazy, because the inside seating wasn't even close to being at occupancy. I might have been crazy, but not in a certifiable way.

I contemplated the odds of getting hypothermia, or frostbite just to avoid sitting in a place where people could stare at me. It's not that I'm some sort of eremite or angsty teen. I just don't want their looks to make me feel bad about myself—I can do that on my own.

Never have I feared death, I feared living life as a failure. The irony is, when you avoid your fears, you become what you avoid. With that thought on the edge of my mind, I succumbed to the warm underbelly that is social interaction.

The host asked if he could take my jacket. As I pulled down the zipper, I remembered my tank top and denied his service in order to save face. This was not the type of place to show off your pale arms, and mine were the palest.

I was led to a seat adjacent to a roaring fireplace. It was a family-sized booth which could easily accommodate five or six people. I felt five or six times worse than I had previously.

"Excuse me, isn't there something a little smaller? At the bar, perhaps?" I asked, noticing all the smaller tables were occupied for "date night."

The host looked at me as if I were asking him for a table shaped like a dinosaur. "We can't bring food to the bar."

I debated substituting my meal calories for more heavy drinking. I was quite hungry, and I was planning on getting a pasta dish, which was about 1,000 calories. *That's about five drinks...*

"The booth will have to do," I said from a place of defeat.

"Someone will be back with the specials."

"Thank you," I said, already thumbing through the Happy Hour menu.

Ever notice how happy people never indulge in Happy Hour? It should be more appropriately called, "Loser Hour, where you drink your problems away." That's how I felt about the matter, anyway.

I shifted uneasily in my seat.

*Where do I put my hands?*

There was so much space to conquer. I bent my knee and draped my arm around an invisible person.

"Sorry for the delay," a busboy said out of nowhere, like a jack-in-the-box, scaring me half to death.

He looked at me with a sense of worry on his face, making me feel exactly how I feared I would—totally pathetic.

I took a menu out of his hand. He proceeded to drop additional menus and place settings at the empty spaces on the table, adding salt onto my already wounded ego.

Instead of drawing more attention to myself and explaining how I was one of those loners—too cool to eat with other human beings—I decided to go with it.

"Only one extra menu," I said, motioning to the person who wasn't next to me.

His head cocked to the side slightly, very confused.

"What? You're not eating?" I said, to my armpit. "That explains your invisible waistline. Never mind. Just the one menu will do."

The busboy slowly collected the other menus, never taking his eyes off my imaginary person.

I should have taken my chances with the outside elements. At least no one would have noticed if I passed away into the cold of night.

While trying to decide if I wanted sausage or fish, I felt a force boring into my subconscious. Someone was staring at me. I never understood how you could almost feel someone's intention from their gaze, like a hidden laser. Real or imagined, in that moment I felt it intensely.

My attention was diverted away from my hunger, though I didn't dare look up.

It was one of those moments where you feel like something is going to happen to you any minute, but that minute passes by, uneventful. You wait the next, expecting the unexpected. Still no change. It's like waiting for the phone to ring. As long as you watch it, that moment will never come. Life lives on its own timeline and doesn't heed to your command.

I could have screamed, but that would have induced more unwanted eyes upon me.

"You only live once," I slurred to myself. Then I thought of a counter to the old saying. *You also only die once.*

Finally, I gathered enough courage to pry my head out from behind my menu and investigate the cause of my feelings.

My eyes met hers instantly. They were big and beautiful, even from across the room. I saw myself differently in that moment. She didn't look puzzled, or scared, or horrified. I felt as if I belonged here, and I didn't dare to blink. Tracing her features, I started to draw her image inside my mind so that I might never forget it. Her hair bounced freely, tickling her shoulders. Although she was clothed in the same uniform as her co-workers, she wore it in a defiant way—somehow saying, "I'm my own person, and I won't conform to your rules." It was a statement I respected. She was fighting the system, while also fighting poverty.

She gave me a small half-smile, which made her whole face come alive. How could something so wonderful spring from looking at me, of all people?

Her smile let out a sadness that only I could understand. Within that small look, it was as if she shared her whole life with me.

She must have had a lonely childhood, like I did. Maybe a loss of a parent or loved one. It couldn't be the loss of her mother. She seemed much too girly to be raised by a single dad.

Believe me, I know how tough it is to grow up without the support system of both parents. Mine got divorced when I was young. They fought about who *had* to take me, not who *got* to keep me. In the end, I lived with my father. He made more money than my mother, and he didn't want to fork over a hefty child support payment—which made good business sense.

I wanted to tell her how much I understood her. How I could never replace the emptiness she had felt her whole life, but maybe, with time, I could make it hurt less.

We stared at each other like it was some sort of childhood competition. I watched her watching me as she blindly wiped down the bar with a rag. She had work ethic—I admired that—especially in a job she was overqualified to perform. I bet she would be happier at home creating wonderful works of art—abstract, yet very telling as to what she went through in this life; painting her pain to cope. Using her art as a way of searching for something invisible, a missing piece to her heart's puzzle. A sentiment to something she never knew she needed. Something that is, undoubtedly, me.

It wasn't a mistake that I ran out of booze, or that the weather was biting. It was fate that I should sit in this huge booth by myself. I felt like all my experiences led me to this moment where everything would change, everything would be glorious. All I had to do was lead myself the rest of the way.

A nervous feeling came over me. Not because I feared getting rejected, but more that I feared being happy, as it has been far too long.

The moment was only too brief, as the busboy asked her a question. She was jostled, as if caught doing something outside her duties as a bartender—which she was, luring me in like a siren, against the crashing waves of my heart.

"Can I take your order, or do you need some more time?" the waiter asked me, chomping on some gum.

I couldn't wait any longer. I had to take her away with me, to spend the rest of our days together.

"Not now," I pushed past the server, knocking his pen out of his hand.

"Rude much?"

Zeroed in on her beauty, nothing else in this world mattered but her and me.

She was even more enchanting as I made my approach. Her smile ignited a fuse within me and I had to talk to her before I exploded—emotionally speaking, of course, or maybe not. Spontaneous human combustion had never been fully researched. This could be the cause. Never one for being the subject of any sort of experiment, I decided I had to talk to her, as if my life depended upon it.

Taking a seat at the end of the bar, I felt somewhat relieved. I inhaled the sweet aroma of her perfume.

"Jasmine," the word blissfully fell out of my mouth. That's what she smelled like. She could have smelled like tea tree, or patchouli, but she had to smell like my favorite. I looked forward to having her scent linger on me when we were apart, while I was missing her.

"Yes? Hey, how did you know my name?" she asked, looking up at me with those bright green eyes.

I couldn't have guessed a more fitting name for my delicate flower, so pure and soft.

"Can I get a drink?" I asked, not wanting to come off as too strong, or crazy.

"Uhh, sure. What can I get you?" she asked, biting her lip in a cute way.

This was my opportunity to convince myself that this was true destiny, not just a figment of my imagination.

"Surprise me," I said, baiting my trap. If it really was kismet, she would know what I liked to drink.

Then a horrifying thought came over me. *What if she gives me a shot of straight alcohol? Would that mean she knows I'm an alcoholic?*

I didn't want her to see me as just an everyday drunkard. *If she truly thinks of me that way, then maybe she doesn't get me at all.*

I never thought about my plan backfiring.

"Do you want anything special or just, like, a casual drink at home?" she asked, looking over the bar's selection.

"Casual, please," I reluctantly said, trying to hide my fidgeting fingers and the jiggling of my leg.

"I got just the thing, sweetie."

*She called me "sweetie."* That's my pet name because of her love of sugar. The joy I give her will only be equaled by her love for chocolate and cakes. Even though she limits her sweets to watch her figure, she never limits her love for me. I will call her Jasmine, not because it's her name, but because it's my favorite and so is she.

"Okay, close your eyes," she said, holding a brown drink on the rocks.

I complied, closing them tightly. Though I couldn't stop my grin from taking up most of my face.

Her cold nails brushed against my cheek as she brought the glass to my lips. She was too close to me. I was having a difficult time keeping myself from kissing her finger. I had to refrain—to be on my best behavior.

Opening my mouth, I let the beverage in—a poor substitute for her lips. The drink was strong, I knew. It smelled familiar to me, though I wasn't certain exactly what it was.

I couldn't wait to tell her all of my thoughts and desires, for our lives to start as if it were the first day of my existence. Today she touched my face, and tomorrow, the rest of my life.

The taste hit my pallet, and my eyes opened wide. "Sherry?"

She nodded with excitement.

I didn't particularly like sherry, it was just what I had left at home.

*Did she smell it on me? Is that why she asked if I wanted a casual drink?* That seems like cheating. Maybe she's got a boyfriend and she aims to cheat on him with me. That's not who I thought she was, but it makes sense. After the loss of her father, she had to cheat on life, as life had cheated her out of a parent. I bet she picked up bartending because she feels better watching other people go from bad to worse, just to feel better about herself.

*How will she feel watching me? Is that why she smiled at me before?*

"Isn't it...old-fashioned?" she said, leaning on her fist.

God, she was cute. Too bad she thought of me as being old, like a father figure. *Why can't she just see me as her equal? Am I really beneath everyone in this world?*

No, I had to get out of my head. She was it, she had to be. This trial wasn't over. I couldn't give up on love, not so soon, anyway.

"How did you know I drank sherry?" I threw out another test.

"You seemed different to me somehow."

That was it. She passed with flying colors. She saw me how I saw her, like an endless dream you look forward to diving into and never waking up from.

I placed her hands inside mine and pulled them close.

Her head dipped, losing its stability.

I couldn't contain myself any longer. "Run away with me, and I'll never let you down, not for a moment!"

She resisted my touch. *Am I coming on too strong? Am I overpowering her? Idiot.*

"That sounds nice, it's just..." she stammered.

I was losing her. I had to think of something quick, to make her see what I felt inside. "I know about your dad, and I will mend your pain. You don't have to grieve him in your art anymore."

"My what?" she asked, pulling her soft hands away from mine. "Do you know my dad?"

It must have been her mother who passed away. *How did I get that wrong?*

"No. It was just a bad call..." I said, covering my mouth. I felt so free talking to her, like I could say anything and she wouldn't judge me, not in the slightest. It was a dangerous feeling, one that could get you into a heap of trouble.

"Look, I thought we were having fun, and you seem nice bu..."

"I am having *so* much fun too," I cut her off.

"It's just that...I'm into women."

Did I hear her right? Maybe it was just a phase from being raised by her father... "Are you sure?"

"Positive."

"Why were you flirting with me?"

"Tips?" she admitted with a cringe.

My mind was blank for the first time in my life. Everything I had ever known was up in the air—except one truth...I had to quit drinking.

The End

# CIRCLES

I do what I say.

I say what I mean.

I'm mean as a way of showing
that I care.

I care way too much to stop.

I stop being myself before
I'm gone.

I'm gone before it ever started.

I started to think I was nobody.

Nobody
cares like I do.

I do what I say...

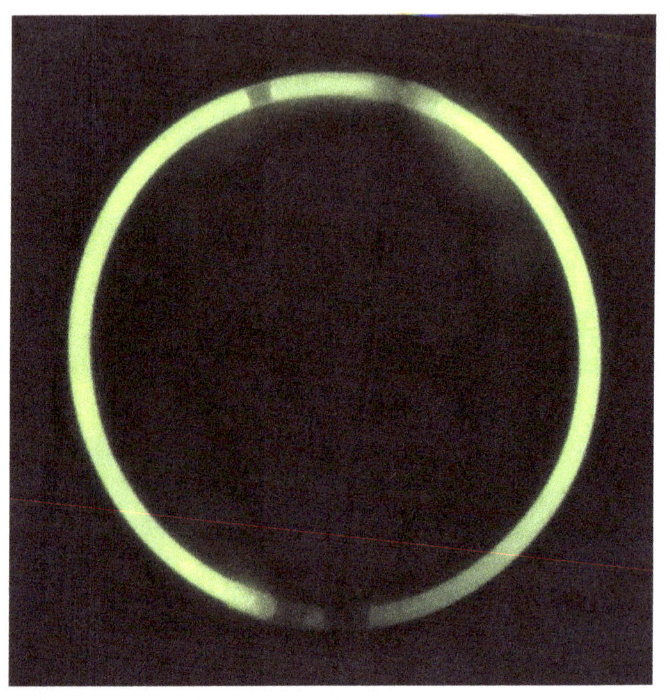

# ILLITERATE SPELLING

A rolling fog conceals the trees and building tops without prejudice; creeping into town like a predator stalking its prey. The sun had shone high in the sky hours prior, without a cloud in sight. Only now, the fiery eye is shrouded by the grey precipitation defusing its rays. This event is no accident, nor a sudden change in the elements. The gas was summoned here by a great power, one whose only match is Mother Nature.

Everyone knows corruption and afflictions, along with the rest of the world's worst terrors, reserve themselves to darkness. Avoiding the light that weakens their shadowy prowess.

Aaron can smell the witchcraft from inside his step van (which he converted into a mobile tarot card reading shoppe) and it smells like misfortune. If it weren't for his current customer, he would have high-tailed it out of there when the mist first manifested itself.

"Can we hurry this up?" Aaron asks abruptly, sitting across the table from his paying customer who is boring him half to death. The mist of impending doom, on the other hand, will attack him completely to death.

"Are you even listening to me?" Gary, a love-struck twenty-year-old, asks, his knees cramped under the fold-out card table.

"I've done your reading twice already. The cards say what they say. I'm not a magic eight ball you can shake until you get the answer you want," Aaron says, adjusting his sparkly headpiece.

Just for the record, his headpiece may look magical and mystical, but it holds no power of its own, other than making Aaron look like an authentic gypsy—which he isn't.

They'd been at it for over an hour now, and Aaron presumes that Gary won't leave until he is told exactly what he wants to hear. In this case, Gary wants to know that his heartbreak is part of a bigger plan, one with a happy ending. But the cards won't reflect any such skipping-down-the-street feelings, not today, not for him.

*"You people* have it so easy. I wish I could be into...you know," Gary says to Aaron with a smirk, tapping his index fingers against each other. He is filled with an over-comfortableness that you don't normally have towards someone you've only known for a few hours.

"No, I don't. What are you implying?" Aaron asks, hoping Customer Gary isn't getting stereotypical on him about his sexual preference.

"You're the psychic, you tell me." His smirk grows even wider, if that is even possible.

"First, I'm not psychic. Do I look that unhinged? Am I putting out that sort of vibe?" Aaron asks, flipping over another tarot card in disgust.

"It's the hat. One hundred percent, the hat."

"It's called a headpiece. And for the record, I'm a reader. There's a difference. A really big one."

"So, you can't see my future? What am I paying you for?" Gary asks, banging his knees against the table as he tries to make a dramatic outburst but fails miserably. "Goddamn it."

"I'm not some quack who thinks they can speak to the dead, if that's what you're implying." Aaron waves his hand over the cards, palms down, studying their meaning. "Like the dead don't have better things to do than speak to the living," he says under his breath.

"I know what you're trying to do. You want to keep this debate open so that I pay you for another hour," Gary says, thinking himself a detective.

"If that were remotely true, why have I been trying to get rid of you for the last half hour?"

"Reverse psychology?" Gary asks, thinking he has figured out his scheme.

"Try again." He reaches down and tosses Gary back his shoes. "This isn't therapy. Would ya put these back on?" Aaron didn't understand why clients insisted on getting overly comfortable before a reading. Always removing tight clothing or jewelry like glasses, belts brassieres, socks and one person even removed her panties. They would even do away with their false body parts, like prosthetics, toupees, eyelashes, nails, teeth, breast padding, even glass eyes. None of this stuff ever influences the cards in the slightest. The only effect it has is on how much Aaron is forced to hide his disgust, which he is becoming a master at.

"Do you have somewhere you need to be?" Gary asks, irritated.

"Bingo," Aaron says, with a finger gun and a wink.

"Fine. What was I saying before?" Gary completely ignores Aaron's plea and directs the focus back upon himself.

"Something about your luck with women?" Aaron recalls, with a sigh.

"Ah, yes. You see, women have this way of weaving their magic inside my mind and soul, and just when I think I'm free, they reel me back in."

"That isn't magic, it's their boobs," Aaron says. He gulps a mouthful of air as he notices the mist seeping under his van outside.

Gary takes a moment to ponder the concept. Or so that is what he intended to do. Instead, he is remembering his ex's chest, which he misses dreadfully.

"I don't have time for this. You need to go, now!"

"What?" Gary says, still entrenched in thought.

"Sorry."

"For a man who doesn't like women, you seem to know a lot about them."

"No one said I didn't like them, they're just not my thing. Also, overstaying my welcome isn't my thing. Personally, I find it rude." Aaron helps Gary lace up his shoes, like you would a child.

"I think you're right. Maybe I should date women with less..." Gary says, reaching his hands out as if cupping his own imaginary mounds.

"That sounds like a plan. I'm glad you, me, we thought of it," Aaron says, nearly pushing him out the door as Gary continues to move his hands back and forth trying to imagine a breast size that would be suitable. As Gary's hands move closer to his body, a scowl forms on his face.

"Wait! What about the cards? Do you think they would approve of this development?" Gary saves himself from being ejected out of the step van by propping his leg against the door frame.

Feeling around inside his long flowing robe, Aaron finds a stray card inside a hidden pocket. It's the Mad Magician card. He licks the back and sticks it on his customer's forehead, not caring about convention or germs. "The universe likes it."

"You really think so?" Gary asks, not wanting to move his hands from the perfect breast size he feels he has discovered.

"Oh yes, it loves that idea. You can keep that as a souvenir. I've got plenty." Aaron always kept one ace up his sleeve for such emergencies. Some may think this act to be a little dishonest, or even consider it fraudulent. Those kinds of people are realists and have a good head upon their shoulders—not typically the type that pays a perfect stranger to shuffle a deck.

Finally hearing what he wants prompts Gary to fork over a wad of small bills as a tip, while he is forcibly exited from the vehicle.

Aaron ignores the chump change, letting the money fall on the floor, making him feel like a stripper or Greek dancer. He is focusing on something much bigger than money...living. Aaron knows from experience that they don't accept paper money in the afterlife, and even if they did, no one is selling extra lives there.

The open door lets mist pour into the van. Gary obliviously staggers through the evil smog, looking for where he parked his car.

The mist darkens and starts to form elongated hands reaching for Aaron. He tries his darnedest to blow it away with a decorative Asian fan. This dissipates the form long enough for him to lock the door tightly.

He moves a velvet blanket and uncovers a large crank which he rapidly cranks like he's stirring a huge caldron, or doing the Cabbage Patch. This awakens a contraption of gears and valves, causing cogs and chains to make a huge racket. The neon sign slides down and turns off, the window shades snap open, and the steps collapse and are stowed in the underbelly of the van.

All the panels on the outside flip from a beautifully illustrated deck of cards into an nondescript white color. Nothing like the color white to repel light, solicitors, and anyone who doesn't take kindly to kidnapping. His place of business is now transformed into a road-ready vehicle.

"Come on. Come on," he says, switching out his tiring arm for the next.

Reaching the last revolution of the crank turns on the engine. He secures the crank into place, and almost trips over himself trying to make it to the driver's seat.

Mist has found another way inside, through the front air vents, and it is flooding in. Aaron slaps each vent closed while switching off the air-conditioning. Too bad for Aaron, who has been perspiring heavily.

This is clearly the dark arts, and he knows exactly how to escape...he needs to find the sun's light for protection.

With his windshield wipers going full tilt, he takes off into the unknown haze. Every obstacle is concealed by the peasoup. Luckily for Aaron, this small town doesn't have many buildings or structures. However, it had lots of fences and shrubbery, emphasis on the word "had."

Aaron is driving blindly through the vapor, with no way of knowing if he is even riding on a road. It feels more like a world paved in Legos. Plowing through the dark fog, he turns on his headlights affording him a few feet of clarity—just enough to see exactly what he is hitting. The U.V.-enhanced bulbs cause the mist to evaporate on contact, but it doesn't take long to re-form and snake back around, giving in to the chase.

"Mailbox!" Aaron cries, as the custom-made depository shatters on the hood. Judging by the black and white splotched wood shards, he figures it was designed to resemble a cow. A letter is lodged under the passenger-side wiper, making the worst possible noise ever as it streaks across his windshield.

Up until ten minutes ago, life was going well for Aaron. About a month back, he figured things were almost too good to be true. Often when that occurs, happenstance tends to arrive and prove you right.

That was the impetus that made him install such anti-evil headlamps in the first place. He was hoping to thwart such an incident. He begins to wonder if buying the unique item may have alerted the evil to his presence, though he quickly shakes off the notion. All that matters now is that the lamps are working, but he knows it isn't going to keep him alive forever as he glances at the nearly empty gas gauge.

Distracted by the letter screeching across his windshield, Aaron bangs on the glass trying to hit exactly when the piece of paper comes his way, although his timing is all off. The high-pitch noise is affecting his judgment, as he would do almost anything to make it stop. Completely ignoring the fact that he is driving aimlessly with little to no visibility, he gets the bright idea of reaching out the window to grab the letter while simultaneously turning on and off the wipers, not realizing that leaving them off would end his torment altogether.

This is what always happens to Aaron when he's flustered; he makes bad decisions which result in more bad things happening. He has many scars to press this point further, but those are tales best saved for trying to impress a date.

Switching his attention between the letter and the control switch leaves no room for Aaron to look at the actual road. If he were seeing the fast-approaching barn, it would be quite easy to avoid. Instead, the barn jumps out of nowhere, and the van crashes through the side wall, stopping him dead in his tracks. Aaron is convinced the barn is part of some teleportation or time travel spell, but the rest of us know the truth.

Violently turning the key, he tries to get the step van started again. Each turn drains the battery more and more, making his protective headlights dimmer with each try.

"Come on, baby," he sweet-talks it, hoping that will make a difference, which in his case almost always works...but not today.

The engine just won't turn over. Pulling the key out of the ignition, he kisses it gently with only goodly thoughts in his mind and tries one final time.

Click. Click. Click. Click.

It won't even pretend to try and start any more. He knows it's over. He rests his head on the steering wheel long enough to plan his next action.

Taunting him and testing his patience, the letter slowly and loudly moves across the cracked windshield. The sound it makes is much worse than claws on a chalkboard, worse than a cat in heat, worse than listening to National Public Radio.

"Darn it! Motherfather, stupid, dark evil dillweeds," he yells while slapping and punching the dashboard, knocking over much of his huge bobblehead collection, which shake their heads most disapprovingly. "What a bunch of bullspit. Good for nothing, shitake mushrooms. Should have gotten a sports car. But no, damn figcakes at the..."

He feels the dark vapor saturating the back of his neck as a coldness courses through him. It has arrived. For years, he has tried to run from his past, but here it is, invading his personal space.

Next to the out-of-date fire extinguisher, he spies his emergency U.V. flashlight box, which reads, "In case of apocalypse, break glass." In one fluid motion, he stands up and with all his might, strikes at the glass.

"Sunny beach!" he yells, feeling as though he may have broken his hand. The glass, however, remains completely intact.

"You were always weak, Aaron Drake," a low, booming voice shakes the whole van with its terrible undertones.

Aaron ignores his pain momentarily, seeing the face that's developing inside the mist in front of him. It has distinctively square features that he recognizes. This is not the apocalypse like he thought. It is far worse—it's his family.

"What do you want, Maliconious?" Aaron asks, his head flopping back as if his neck suddenly became weak, while rolling his eyes.

"You need to return home this instant," the mist demands.

"No. You need to buy me a new van, or conjure one, whatever it is you do," Aaron says, twirling his fingers upward. "Like, poof."

"Dearest nephew, I thought you were against all types of mysticism. You could..."

"Not when I am the one who benefits from it," he interrupts, walking through the misty face, turning its words into inaudible mumblings.

A moment later, the face reforms, looking eviler than before, if that were even possible.

"This is not a game. It's about Bethakey."

Aaron pauses, for more than just dramatic effect.

"Or have you forgotten your own mother?"

"I'm thinking..." Aaron says, while puttering around, hopelessly trying to put his work/home/van back together.

It isn't strange that he is estranged from his family, seeing as Aaron never wanted to take part in the family business. His mother is a powerful witch, and she was the hardest part for him to turn his back on. He is trying to remember exactly how he left it with her. Did he have the last word, or did she? It might not seem important to some, but to Aaron, it was everything.

"Don't take too long, or there might not be anything left to remember her by," the mist threatens.

"What do you mean?" Aaron asks, holding a decapitated head of a bobble.

"She has slipped away into the lightness."

"How?"

"The pain of losing her favorite son was just one of many tribulations that led her to her final departure. She ultimately succumbed to burn..."

Aaron throws the head of the bobblehead through the mist, distorting his next words.

"...steak," the mist finishes.

"No, it can't be!" Aaron remembers how careful she was about only purchasing fire-retardant clothing. For a witch, getting burned at the stake was not just humiliating, the fire ignites the magic that flows through a witch's blood causing internal combustion as well. It is by far the worst way to go, and the main fear that keeps Aaron from taking part in the family business.

Aaron can't hide his emotional strife any longer. This is the worst possible news.

"Who was it? An angry mob? Republicans?"

"So, you will come back to fulfill your duties?"

"Yes, fine. Just tell me who to hurt and I'll..." Aaron scans his van for a weapon to maim someone with.

"Johnny's."

"Who's Johnny? I'm so going to...do bad things to him." Aaron's knuckles crack as he makes two tight fists.

"Johnny's is not a who, it's a where."

"Okay, now you're just going over the top with being all ominous," Aaron says, dropping his hands.

"Johnny's Steakhouse. It's quite tasty, well worth dying for."

"Why would a restaurant want to burn a witch? Unless that's their secret recipe...is it?"

"No, no. She choked on burnt steak. Wasn't I clear about that?"

"You kind of cut out during that part." Feeling defeated, Aaron sighs deeply then stops suddenly realizing that he just breathed in some of the mist. "I'm..." Aaron erupts into a coughing fit. "I..." He repeatedly slams his fist against his chest to cease his hacking.

"Will you cut it out!" Maliconious, the mist face, says.

Aaron nods, catching his breath.

"I'm opening a portal now."

"I can't unleash a can of revenge upon a steakhouse. What do you want me to do, give it a bad review, send back food, forget to leave a tip?"

"It doesn't matter what we want or what you want, you already agreed!" Maliconious says, his booming laughter echoes.

Aaron had been tricked by the dark law before. *You should never agree to anything unless you get something in return. Any agreement is permanently binding.* Agreement is a major part of the dark arts, and without consent, most magic is simply a party trick. Vampires and ghosts adhere to this rule. It's amazing what is invisible to your mind when you don't agree it is true. It's this one fundamental that keeps the world from going into utter chaos.

Housewives and BBQ dads in hometown suburbia will never bear witness to the strange and unusual, because they are unwilling to think outside the Pandora's box. Therefore, in turn, they're protected from it by the light.

Aaron never had that luxury, he was born in darkness. He was never able to determine fact from fiction because, to him, fiction was always fact. He tried to get brainwashed years ago. It was a desperate act of a teenager, an attempt to forget his past. Unfortunately, Aaron was raised with real magic and didn't believe in the power of hypnosis. Thus, he was impervious to its effects, one of the many drawbacks to being raised the way he was. He couldn't ignore it any more than a blind man can ignore traffic.

"I'll go, but can...you know...to the van?" Aaron asks with a wink.

"You should have proposed that clause before giving me your full consent."

"Dagnabbit. Where's the fudging portal?"

Maliconious lets out an amused chuckle.

"Where?"

A swirly gas tendril slithers through the air, leading to the rear of the van.

Aaron follows it directly to the very spot he feared, inside his toilet. He flinches, focusing more on the skid marks that Gary didn't have the decency to wipe out than the magical portal inside the bowl.

"Just let me..." Aaron says, reaching for the bristle brush.

Before he can do a little housekeeping, he is sucked in the toilet and through a dimensional gateway, void of time and space. The gateway is known as The Void of Truth. Here there are no ups and downs, rights or wrongs, or "free gifts with purchase."

Before Aaron can marvel at its glory, he's teleported to a restroom he remembers all too well.

He is home and completely wet with toilet water. The bathroom holds no shower or tub. It's more the size of a closet than a room. Nevertheless, Aaron makes good use of its name. He spends the next half hour washing his body with hand soap and drying himself with toilet paper. After chicken-picking the last fiber of T.P. out of his stubble, he puts on a dark expression before reintroducing himself to his former life, the one he tried so hard to leave behind.

Exiting the bathroom refreshed, his aura has a majestic gleam to it, almost like it too had been cleansed. If the experience wasn't so devastatingly gross, he might consider doing this more often.

A long line of red-robed cultists has formed outside the door waiting for him to finish his preparation. Each of their faces is shrouded by the shadow cast from their dark hood. One might suspect them to be some demonic clones, if it weren't for how they each differed in height and weight.

Aaron averts his eyes from the cloaked figures thinking they all seem a little bit pissed. Each one standing in silence, their judging arms crossed like a pretzel, except for one in the middle, who can't help but shuffle uneasily while pulling on his crotch like a boy-child does when he has to go pee-pee in the potty.

Out of nowhere, a humorous thought enters his mind, *robes don't have any zippers. Do they have to lift the bottoms up to urinate?*

The first cultist enters the bathroom and slams the door behind him, confirming Aaron's suspicion about their mood. As a chorus of uncomfortable groans starts up like an undead group of Christmas carolers, Aaron figures that he needs get out of there before things get much worse and much wetter.

He makes his way past the ancient Cathedral of Sacrifice, hoping to pass by unnoticed. This of course is impossible in a place such as this with gypsies, fortunetellers, and general know-it-alls about.

Aaron receives no happy waves or curious smiles from the prestigious guests that have already started to pour into the old hall. All he catches are a bunch of gaunt looks from generally miserable people.

What did he expect, "Welcome to hell. I'll be your best friend"? You don't generally see pixies, fairies and godmothers trading magical tidbits with witches, warlocks, and magicians. One could safely say that they dislike one another, whereas others might say they're mortal enemies. Aaron, on the other hand, thought of the aforementioned solely as stuck-up prima donnas (as opposed to the real Madonna who was quite down to earth and a second-generation witch, in her own right).

Aaron responds to their glares by scrunching up his nose, while showing a teensy bit of his gnashing teeth. He resembles a chipmunk showing displeasure after smelling some rank flatulence, if a chipmunk can smell such a smell.

"Excuse you," a deep voice says, sounding as if a lifetime of beer and cigarettes has conditioned it to the point of perpetual laryngitis.

Aaron follows his ears, only to find that he does not recognize the wizened woman standing before him. She holds her importance on her stiff shoulders, along with an elegant house cat—a Scottish fold to be exact.

He knows that she is a spell caster of great importance due to the living fur draped around her neck. Each witch who has reached the upper echelons of a coven is always noticeable by their feline accessories. Siamese, Sphinx and Bengals were a few that Aaron had seen proudly displayed around a high-witch's neck, purring and adoring the attention just as much as the witches themselves. Lower members of the sect had rodents biting on their ear lobes, and even lower still had the aid of insects to glam up their attire, but for the most part, they just bugged everyone around them.

The woman turns her nose up at Aaron. "Well, I certainly..."

Aaron has no idea what he did to offend her. "What did I do wrong..." Before he can finish his own thought, Aaron interrupts himself spying her exquisite cats-eye broach, which really brings her outfit together. "Oh, so pretty!"

Reaching for the gem-filled masterpiece, he is instantly held in place by a magic witchy power emanating from her pruned hand. One finger is twice the size of the rest and acting as a kind of wand.

"You will learn your place with me, insolent half-brain," she says, and her cat-cessory lets out a "meow" in agreement.

Aaron suddenly feels detached from his body as if looking at himself through a window, like a stalker or a hungry hobo watching you eat.

*Corn nuts!*

He loses all control over himself, like a marionette who just had its strings cut off.

She twists and turns her long finger causing a hideous smile to grow upon his vacant face.

*That looks horrible. Is that what I look like? I'm never going to smile again,* Aaron rethinks his whole perception he had about himself.

"I am Faramila, your new master. You shall serve me until I die, yes?"

Aaron's head nods slowly. To him, it looks almost sarcastic, at least that is how justifies it to himself.

"Splendid. I must warn you, I'm immortal," she says with a horrendous cackle.

His body kneels, starting a low bow, while his spirit starts to distance itself from it even more, as if giving up on this life altogether. He is losing himself to a dumb witch with a fantastic broach.

His body slowly leans towards her leather shoe as she lifts her dress.

*No, anything but that...*

Even detached, he can taste the snake-oil she uses to polish her footwear, as his tongue slowly makes its way up to her boot.

"Excuse the intrusion, High Coveness," a man says as he approaches them.

"Never interrupt me while I'm playing."

"Normally I wouldn't, but in this case, I must," the man says with an apologetic bow.

"Get on with it," she says, moving her tongue around as if the very words taste bad inside her mouth.

"May I present Aaron, Bethakey's miscreant exile, who is here to pay his respects for your coronation ceremony."

Aaron remembers the man's voice, it's the same warlock from the mist—his annoying uncle. Although Maliconious is proving quite useful for once.

Like a bolt of lightning Aaron returns to his body mid lick. He feels white leg hairs tickling his cheek. He shutters and quickly launches from the floor to his feet in one leap.

"Ah, Bethakey never spoke an offspring," Faramila says, offering her frail hand for him to kiss, as if he hadn't just nearly gotten to second base with her shoe.

Busy wiping his tongue clean, Aaron almost misses his opportunity for revenge. Before the moment passes, he grabs her hand with his wet one and shakes it, ignoring her gesture completely.

Feeling the dampness, she angrily raises her long finger, a storm brewing inside her eyes.

Aaron feels that she may be overreacting a smidge. What is the difference between slobbering on one extremity over another? Nevertheless, poking the hornet's nest does give him the satisfaction he desired.

"Faramila, darling, there will be time for that *after* the ceremony," Maliconious reassures.

"There will be no such time for that! Not after, during, or otherwise," Aaron says, reclaiming his hand and wiping it on his shirt, as if her hand made it dirtier.

"After then," she says, calming her rage with patience.

"No!" Aaron scowls.

"Quite." Maliconious smiles at her.

"I'm only here for the refreshments, then I'll be on my way, right?" Aaron says.

"Precisely. After the coffin cake, you may depart," Maliconious says, putting his arm around Aaron as they part ways with Faramila. "After," he whispers back to her, like his voice is a paper airplane containing a secret note.

"Yes, delightful," she hisses.

"Yuck fou both!"

Maliconious shakes his head left and right while raising his eye brows as if Aaron is imagining things.

"Whatever, let's just not talk...about this or anything else...ever again."

"Suit yourself." Maliconious leads Aaron down the Corridor of Destiny. Both sides of the meandering hallway are lined with portraits of old, immortalizing the visages of past high priestesses. With each generation, they cast a spell to stretch the hallway to accommodate the newest painting. Each masterpiece is more grandiose than the last, as if there is a competition among the deceased.

Bethakey's painting is larger than life. Aaron's neck cracks as he takes pause to admire the gigantic artwork. The artist did a superb job of making her look truly four-dimensional. Her hair moves with the changing seasons within the magical paint. It even smells like her. She had a very distinct aroma, like a bubble of pure duck farts.

"Down here," Maliconious says, not slowing his unique heel-to-toe walk.

Aaron hurries to keep up, making a "clip-clop" sound with his mouth, mimicking his uncle's stride.

They circle down the stone staircase until they reach the crypt. The tunnels are filled wall to wall with coffins and skeletons alike. It's like the worst possible episode of "Hoarders" you could imagine.

"Why are we down here?" Aaron asks.

"Shh," Maliconious says, looking up.

Red-eyed, sharp-toothed vampires hang from the crypt ceiling, stirring at the sound of his voice.

Aaron rolls his eyes, shakes his head, and repeats his question quieter this time, "Why are we down here exactly?"

"Your mother spent her whole life servicing the coven, and her death left a couple of spells in limbo, if you will."

"Why not just raise her from the dead long enough to cancel their effects?" Aaron asks, remembering how his mother used to reawaken ancient family members to celebrate the Day of the Dead and other holidays of note. Surely it isn't out of the realm of possibility for his uncle, even as a mere warlock.

"We're trying to distance ourselves from zombies. Their appetites are quite the nuisance. Besides, we're already over our headcount for the festivities, and the caterers are on the verge of a total culinary apocalypse."

Aaron suspects that there are bigger issues at play here, but he quickly tosses that concept out of his mind. Like littering in Mexico, it was somebody else's problem. "You know what? I don't care about your little world and all the drama that comes with it. Just tell me what you need, and I'll do it so that I can get on with my life."

"Good to hear." Maliconious stops and places both hands on Aaron's shoulders. "During the ceremony, you will be called upon to perform a ritual of no contest. This will be the moment you must cut your palm with Lemon Blade and..."

"Wait, what's a Lemon Blade? It sounds *really* sting-y."

"Oh no, it is just a name, like Excalibur. You have nothing to fear."

"How deep? Can I do a little prick?" Aaron asks, pinching his fingers together leaving little room between them.

"A single drop will suffice."

"Okay, that's manageable. What then?"

"Take that insignificant drop of blood and..." He takes a deep breath and finishes his sentence twice as fast, "...wipe it on Faramila's forehead, denouncing any and all claim you have on the coven, past present or future. And that's that."

"What was that bit you mumbled?"

"Don't be nervous, you'll do just fine," Maliconious says trailing off deeper into the crypt.

"Warlocks." *Don't agree to anything,* he reminds himself to not make the same mistake twice.

Aaron follows his uncle like anyone surrounded by blood thirsty killers, constantly checking over his shoulder and his shoulder's shoulder. His paranoia goes away once they reach the end of the crypt. Lying on top of an ornate stone sarcophagus is his deceased mother surrounded by black candle light. The dark flames create darkness instead of light. This allows him to see with his wizard eyes instead of his material ones.

Bethakey hasn't aged a day since he saw her ten years ago. In fact, she looks even younger than he. She would look beautiful and peaceful if it weren't for her expression—her neck tightened, eyes bugging out, her hands grabbing at her throat.

Aaron takes a closer look and spies something peculiar lodged inside her mouth. With pinched fingers he manages to pry a piece of meat from her throat, somehow thinking removing it will bring her back.

"Burnt steak, eh?" Aaron says.

"It's a killer."

"Is she going to stay like this forever?"

"Sadly, yes." Malconious snatches the charred object of her demise from Aaron's grasp and quickly pops it into his own mouth.

"No, that's not a good idea!" Aaron cringes upon hearing the saliva sloshing inside his uncle's blissful mouth. "How old is that?"

Chomping on the morsel like it is jerky, "It's still good," Malconious says with the mouthful.

"You know it killed a person, hello?" Aaron says, pointing as his mother's cold corpse.

"You want a taste?" he asks, pulling a chewed-up bit out of his pursed lips.

"No, thank you!" Aaron can't help but gag at the concept of sharing anything out of his uncle's mouth, let alone his dead mother's.

"Death never tasted so good. I stand by my earlier statement, 'well worth dying for,'" Maliconious admits.

Aaron hopes his uncle would choke on the steak just so he won't have to hear his loud eating any longer. "This is why. This is exactly why I left," Aaron says to his dead mother as if she were still alive to hear his words.

"I'll leave you two alone," Maliconious says, licking his fingers loudly as he walks down the tunnel.

"This is not normal, Ma. I've seen normal, and it's simple and great. No A.B.C. death steak, cranky bloodsuckers, or toilet portals. Just mall shopping, keeping up appearances, and TV—lots and lots of cod-damn, boring television—and I love it. Not like how I said I loved your hair when you permed it, because under full disclosure, Ma, it was just okay. And another thing..." Aaron stops himself from saying anything else he may regret when he meets her in the afterlife. He places his hand over his eyes and wipes them down, starting over.

"I'm sorry. We both said things we didn't mean." Aaron places hand over her eyes and gently pulls them closed.

Her lids flip open like a spring.

Once more, he tries to make her look less horrific. They snap open even faster this time. He feels her death pulling at his body, trying to draw him into it.

Aaron steps back quickly and notices that his uncle has fully escaped the crypt, leaving him alone with the departed.

Aaron pulls some sunglasses out of his pocket.

"Nuckin' futs," he exclaims, noticing a crack in the frames.

He places the broken glasses over his late mother's blood-shot eyes, making her look slightly less horrifying and slightly more humorous. "You were always a cool mom," he admits.

Aaron kisses his fingers and holds them above her gaping mouth, which resembles that of someone having a stroke. "I'll make you proud, just this once," he whispers inside her ear.

His words bounce around inside her head before repeating themselves from out of her open mouth.

"See, just when I think we're having a moment, something totally deranged ruins it." Aaron turns away from his mother and makes his way out of the terrifying crypt.

Guests and the magically inclined are already pouring into the hall like a casting call for trick-or-treaters. Never has Aaron seen a larger collection of oddly-dressed awkwardness in his life, and he attends Comic Con on a regular basis.

Packed shoulder to shoulder, he crams himself into the herd—headfirst into the congestion—without really knowing where to go. In the sea of supernatural marvels, Aaron cannot trace the musky aroma that is nearly choking him. He tastes perspiration he can only describe as the sweat of a thousand unwashed pits. As an act of survival, he tries to distance himself from it. His first guess would be the wereboar two people away from him, which is a little were-ist on his part, but anyone could be a suspect in present company. Taking in another whiff, he reflects on how it *is* really starting to feel like Comic Con.

Aaron suddenly feels a "tap, tap" tapping on his shoulder. He attempts to turn around, but he's wedged between two animated trees. He manages to catch a glimpse of the hand's owner without his head popping off his shoulders, though it feels as though it's still a possibility.

It's Reddric, a childhood friend, only now he has two heads on his body instead of just the one. "Hey, Red, I like the new look," Aaron says with a squished wave, as if his arm belongs on a tyrannosaurus rex.

"Thanks! It's the same look really, just more of it," Red says, tousling the hair on both his heads. "Do you want to go somewhere to catch up? Somewhere less..."

"Putrid?"

"We were going for mutant-y, but that works too."

Aaron gives his friend(s) an inquisitive look, wondering if Red should be judging mutants when he has his own abnormality going on. "How about the kitchen?"

"Alright! We'll meet you there."

Aaron climbs one of the animated trees to catch a break from the herd.

"Don't tread on me," the construct says.

"Really? That's the best you've got, 'don't tread on me'? I would have gone with 'leaf me alone' or maybe 'you're barking up the wrong tree," Aaron says, giving the being a lesson in wit as he climbs.

"I will rip out your insides and use them to fertilize my young," the tree threatens.

"You win," Aaron says, swinging off its branch. A couple awkward bumps and flying elbows later, Aaron finds himself surrounded by cooks and wait staff who look so stressed that they're about to explode. "Man, Maliconious wasn't kidding," Aaron says.

Reddric arrives at the rendezvous spot shortly thereafter.

Aaron goes in for an embrace, though he doesn't know which side to go to. When someone has two heads there isn't much shoulder room to lean over.

Instead of hugging, Red grabs his arm as a greeting. "It's been far too long. How have you been holding up?"

"I must tell you that I'm out of the family business."

"We feel like we knew that," Red's left head says.

Aaron leans back and accidentally touches a hot stove. "Kitty whiskers!!"

"Are you okay?" Red's right head asks.

He blows on his fingers, hoping that will ease his pain somehow. "I'm surviving. I mean, I got a tarot truck," Aaron says, not quite sure which head he should look at. Both spoke to him. He wonders if it would be rude to give one more attention over the other.

"We were referring to your hand."

"Oh, that's fine too."

"A tarot truck? Do you sell coffee and cakes out of it?" each head asks a question.

"Yup, you caught me. I know, very hipster of me." Aaron now wonders how perfectly bland he must seem to Two-Head Red.

"It just strikes us as odd, guessing someone's future instead of casting a quick spell and knowing the answer."

"I like the gamble. What's the fun in always knowing the answers of things?"

"How about the thrill of never being wrong?"

"That doesn't sound fun at all..."

"Why'd you leave anyway?"

"Look, it isn't their appearance or passion for sin that bothers me, it's that they're so booooorring."

Red's abrupt laughter confirms the ridiculousness of Aaron's statement.

"Okay fine, the normal world is much tamer in its own right. It also has less rules. You can just sit around and not have to worry about necrotic plagues, poltergeist problems, or extermination," Aaron says with a smile.

"Fair enough," Red says, stealing a sample from a passing by tray of finger foods. "So, what brings you back here?" he asks, gnawing on a knuckle sandwich.

The smile quickly fades from Aaron's face.

"Sorry, our mistake...of course we know why you're here. What we meant to say was, how long are you here for?"

"Just the service. I'm going to watch them crown the new b...witch, Faramila, and be on my way," Aaron says, slightly getting in front of a chef.

"Get out of my way unless you want to be part of my soup stock!" the chef says.

Aaron jumps to the side faster than a sprung jack-in-the-box.

"Faramila? Are you sure? She's a total harridan," Red asks, not missing a beat.

"She wouldn't be my first choice, but then again, it isn't my choice," Aaron says, still keeping his eyes on the crazed-looking chef who hasn't unlocked his gaze from his own since the incident.

"That's the thing, it's always the consanguineous choice, which means you."

"I know why I don't like the old bat, but what do you have against her?"

"Well, your mother did a lot of good for humanity and witchfolk alike, setting a balance of peace. I fear that Faramila wants to undo that progress and wage war among the gift-less. Faramila always opposed your mother, fighting her tooth and nail."

"I thought her life's work was giving up on me?"

"This isn't about you. This is bigger than you," Red became serious in tone.

This is not at all good for Aaron who doesn't want to get dragged into this world. He doesn't care one way or another who the queen of witch-land is, he only cares to never lick another person's shoe as long as he shall live.

"What would you do?" Aaron asks the right head.

"As a warlock, we're powerless to stop it. Only a witch can harness enough darkness to stop Faramila," the left head responds.

"No, I mean, if you were me?"

"These are evil, spiteful people with huge egos and a penchant for revenge. We don't think we would have come back at all if we were you."

"I agree, coming back wasn't my brightest moment. Even still, that doesn't help me in the slightest. What would you do if you were me *now,* in this situation?"

"We would kill ourselves. That would take extreme suffering out of the equation."

"I'm not going to kill myself!"

"Not dressed like that you're not." The two heads bump into each other in a sort of head-five.

Aaron looks himself up and down, trying to figure out the extent of the insult. Maybe his ruffled top with a sun/moon pattern on it is a little much, but it's his work attire. It isn't like he dresses like this while he's not working. Except, he does work every day. And the outfit does have a comfort level equal only to a sweat-pant jumpsuit.

Aaron never remembered Red indulging in such raillery. Maybe it's the extra head of his. "Now, I have to ask. How did you get the extra weight on your shoulders? Did you lose a bet? Eat something bad? Were you behind in your work and cast a spell to 'get yourself ahead'?"

"No, no, and definitely not."

"So, tell me?" Aaron is so focused that he doesn't even notice a giant clam is starting to eat a line cook whole.

"There's nothing to tell, really. We had a lump and it itched a lot. One day we popped it, thinking we found the mother of all zits, and instead we discovered an eye ball looking back at us. Soon, we found that we could control it, and eventually more of it came out until..."

"Ta da!" the other head finishes the sentence.

"Nothing to tell? That is quite a tell-able story. Did you find yourself any...smarter?"

"Smarter than you. We still can't believe you came back here."

"Alright. Why don't you come up with a plan, geniuses?"

Both heads turn to each other and start whispering and nodding. They speak so fast it almost sounds like bees buzzing.

Aaron hoists himself on top of the stainless-steel countertop while he waits patiently. He watches the kitchen havoc ensuing around them. They're pulling ingredients out of portals, growing live animal flesh to enormous sizes on the backs of rats, and double dipping their tasting spoons (gross).

"Okay, we've got something," Red's heads say.

"That was quick."

"The element of surprise. We need to know what spells you can cast, but..."

"I can't cast any spells."

"What do you mean? Your mother was the most powerful witch...not in the world, but certainly in this town, maybe in all of North America—excluding the bible belt. Those guys can really cast."

"I was a rebel, and I rebelled."

"So, you can't do this?" Red twinkles his fingers back and forth producing electric energy between them until mosquitos appear out of nowhere.

Aaron tries to mimic Red's movement exactly, but he ends up looking like Pauly Shore doing the weasel. "What can I say, I dropped out of spell class."

"Are you telling us that you never got ordained as a warlock?"

"I avoided it, like raisins in cookies."

Both heads continue to debate amongst themselves, leaving Aaron back to his new favorite reality show, the real "Hell's Kitchen."

The chef he almost bumped into is still locked on Aaron while sharpening his butcher knife. Aaron decides to start a staring contest between himself and the deranged chef. This only makes the chef's spiteful eyes pop even more out of his skull.

Aaron wonders if perhaps by him holding his birthright, he may be inciting all this hatred towards himself. It could be classic jealously among the wicked.

The chef starts to lobotomize the heads of lettuce, never looking down. He accidentally chops off his own hand and blood sprays everywhere. Fast moving leeches launch out of boiling pots just to get a taste.

"I am always making matters worse," Aaron thinks out loud.

"No, this might be a good thing. We came up with a new plan. A much better plan." Red gives Aaron a sly nod, urging secrecy to their conversation. "You'll go up in front of everyone as planned, but instead of crowning Faramila, you'll pick someone else, undoing the whole ceremony."

"So, I don't have to cut myself?" Aaron asks, wincing at the sight of the chef trying to swat away all the leeches currently eating him alive.

"Is that *all* you took away from our scheme?"

"Hey, I'm attached to my body, and I don't take kindly to putting holes in it. Also, leeches...they suck."

"Cutting yourself with the dagger will release the power inside your blood and grant it to a new bloodline. That's what she wants, but rest assured, we're going to stop it."

"How exactly? You sort of glossed over the part where we overpower a powerful witch with a spell school dropout."

"When you take the stage, instead of ordaining Faramila, you will read from your mother's book of spells. Doing so will bring forth the next high priestess for you to consecrate. They'll never expect it, and...and...it will be beautiful."

"This all seems very far-fetched, but if you say so. I am willing to do anything that doesn't involve that Faramila...and her shoes."

"It's much farther fetched that you can possibly know, and that is exactly why it is going to work," Red says, starting to dance a little, unleashing his excitement for the plan he has carefully concocted.

"What do we do now?" Aaron asks, turning his head away from the sous chef who is trying to scare the leeches away by inducing himself to barf acid at them.

"You need to steal your mother's spell book while we get our things and do a little research. Meet us in an hour at..."

"The old chapel?" Aaron interjects.

"Okay, that'll do. Do you remember where it is?" Red's heads ask, knowing that there is a protective ward hiding it from the naked eye.

"Yes, mother used to hide Easter brains and chocolate crosses there for me to find."

Red closes his eyes and squishes up his faces, trying to find an appropriate response that won't make his old friend feel at all insulted. "That's not exactly normal, even among spell casters."

"It was one of our traditions that I actually enjoyed."

"Just meet us there...without the brains, if you please."

^^^

Making his way through the old graveyard brought back childhood memories—digging holes, playing hide-and-creep and blood-red rover. Instantly the tune repeats inside his head, "Blood-red rover, blood-red rover, send a flaming spear on over."

It wasn't *all* bad growing up in a place of wickedness and witchery. Normal for him was mixing potions, crafting voodoo dolls and performing blood rituals. He never understood what other peoples' standards for normalcy were until he left this place. That was when his whole perspective changed. He had felt as if he was lied to his whole life, so much so that even the lies had lies, but that was also a lie.

To be fair, facts never exist in a place like this. When you can change fiction into fact-tion there is no point in debating anything, because it can change in a moment, or never have existed in the first place.

Following the secret instructions marked on tombstones, Aaron arrives at the elusive, old chapel, way before Reddric. What Aaron didn't tell his childhood friend was that his mother's spell book was always kept here. It was more than him being efficient, it was also him being lazy. Fine, it was manipulation—and the only power Aaron has, seeing as he is devoid of any spell abilities of his own. Like how a blind person adapts to the loss of sight, Aaron has adapted to getting what he wants without magic.

The chapel doors open on their own, or at least that's how it would appear to someone who isn't "in the know." Aaron is though and greets the specter that haunts this old place, "Hello, Raymond. I see you're still at it. Well, I don't 'see' but...you know."

In response, the stained-glass windows rattle and shake in excitement.

Aaron sees a trail of footprints marring the dust layer on the hardwood floor. Feeling as if time is rewinding, he steps inside each footprint leading himself deeper into the chapel. He looks back and notices that with each step he takes, the footprint disappears upon meeting his foot, as if he is undoing the past with each step forward.

Following the path, he arrives at a thick glass case surrounded by more black candles. There it is, her life's work, her manifesto of wizardry, her dearest of diaries.

The gold latch lifts, opening right up, by the invisible hand of Raymond.

Never had Bethakey allowed Aaron to even gaze upon its awesome power. He was deemed unworthy, untrusting, and always had "sticky, little fingers." He knows that opening it now is quite unforgivable.

His sticky, little fingers trace the rough pentagram outlines and demonic symbols on the cover. He cracks open the spine, and the book begins to sing a melody that sounds as if it is being sung by a toothless, tongueless banshee. Haunting and disturbing, it is also beautiful. Each page he flips through holds a tune all its own. He plays with the book as if it were a musical instrument, going back and forth between the pages. Finally, he has the idea to flip all the pages at once. Doing so brings out a word he understands. "Aaron," it sings slowly.

The book just spoke to him, or was it her from the darkness of beyond? In either case, he doesn't want to play with the thing any longer. It is far beyond his realm of understanding, and he knows that making one false move could open a portal to a demon's lair, or worse—church.

"Good, you found it," he hears Red's voices echo from the end of the chapel.

"Aaron," the book says again, this time without the aid of him flipping the pages.

"Quiet, you," he whispers to the heavy tome, holding it to his chest as he watches Red make his way to him.

"What did we miss?" Red asks, his arms filled from waist to chin with fabric and books.

"Is it just me, or is it weird being raised with the dead?" Aaron asks, looking around for any signs of Raymond, hoping not to offend the old, ghastly guy.

"It could be worse, you could be raised from the dead," Red jokes.

Aaron shakes his head, wondering why he ever expected a serious answer from Reddric. "So, what did you uncover? Anything besides your bad jokes?"

"Believe it or not, we do have a book of humorous antidotes."

Aaron did believe it, though he didn't believe it was the time to start that conversation. "Hit me with all you've got."

Red let loose his arms, dropping his load everywhere. "A lot of interesting information, really, but we don't think you'll like it."

"Are you trucking kidding me? I like information as much as the next guy."

"Listen here," Red picks up a small pocket-sized book that appears to be handmade. "Musali batolo, fa..."

"I can stop you right there. I don't speak Wickery," Aaron says, referring to the dialect of witches and warlocks.

"You're killing me worse than an alien at a science convention. Didn't your mother teach you anything?"

"Haci, dona malicfus," Aaron recounts the only phrase he remembers.

"Mommy, I make pee-pee? That can't be the extent of your knowledge of the scared words."

"I'm afraid so."

Red can't dignify that with even a glance and presses a nose back inside the tiny book. He starts again, this time translating the text into English for his deprived compatriot, "A warlock's place is in the black heart. His affections and wants to determine his design. The true power comes from deep within the wants—the richness of desire, and the boldness of taste. Whereas, a witch isn't so often noticeable by its pointy features, a warlock's wand isn't any less pointy. Though a witch will abide by the same laws of self, warlocks may differ not in appearances, nor the mark of the title, only the claim."

"I understood the words you said, but I don't get why you said them," Aaron admits.

"Let us translate it once more, this time into idiot."

"Thank you. That would be great."

"Are you a warlock or a witch?" Red asks, holding up two garments, one in each hand. The left is a thick velvet robe customary of any respectable acolyte. The right is a thin, wiry dress. Its sheer layers combine metal with fabric.

"I'm a Warlock. Have you gone mad?" Aaron asks, as he reaches for the red robe.

"Not so fast. The words state that the design of a warlock lies in the wants. So, think about it. Are you a warlock who pines after the power and body of a witch, or are you a witch who dominates and devours her warlocks?"

"First, I'm offended that you are trying to refer me to as a 'her.'"

"It's not in the way you identify yourself with a pronoun. It's in the desire. Who do you prefer to warm your bed?"

"To be honest, I've never really had an opportunity to be with a witch. I guess I'd prefer a warlock, but..."

"No buts."

"How can I be into warlocks with butts off the table?"

"We're being serious. This is law, written in the ink of blood. You must choose for yourself. Look honestly and make a choice." Red holds both garments up higher, while each head tries to urge him to its respective side. One head whispers, "Warlocks are cool man, join us." While the other head says, "Say 'yes' to the dress."

Aaron closes his eyes and imagines a beautiful woman emerging from the salty sea, her shimmering clothes almost translucent if the moonlight were to catch her just right. Even within his own imagination he tries to close his eyes to obscure himself from her strange curves.

Without instruction, his mind transposes the woman into an equally attractive male who consumes all of Aaron's attention, as he eagerly tries to catch a better glimpse of the man's hidden body. He knows what is concealed underneath, though it doesn't curb his desire to confirm his suspicions.

"Aaron, are you okay? Do we need to dumb this down to toddler level for you?"

Snapping out of his fantasy, Aaron snatches the dress. "Just because I like men, don't think that I like to do this sort of thing. I'm not a drag queen!"

"You're a drag witch."

"Reddric, you're becoming a real drag with your jokes," Aaron gives into the ploy and starts to remove his tarot-card garb behind a pillar.

"Just put on the dress, and we promise we won't laugh at you."

"Don't make promises you know you can't keep." Slipping off his clothes and into the thin, scratchy dress makes Aaron feel ridiculous, self-conscious, and even powerful. He steps out of the shadows with his arms modestly covering his body. The gown is a sleek cut, and fits firmly to his frame.

"Looking good, Erin," Red says, trying his best to hide his smirk.

"You said!" Aaron scolds with a pointing finger. Even that small motion has power over Red's hysteria, which is about to burst from the seams. Instead, Red feels a calm strike through him as his laughter deflates.

"I can feel it. You've made the right choice. Even an untrained witch has more power than a skillful warlock."

"But, is the dress *really* necessary?"

"If you cannot accept the dress, how are you going to accept your place within the coven?"

"Let's just get this over with so that I can go back to...anything else."

Reddric draws a circle around Aaron with a red liquid he takes from a glass-blown bottle.

"Is blood always necessary in all rituals?" Aaron asks, sticking out his tongue.

"It's not blood, though it is a common mistake. It's only Rock-a-Dile Red Kool-Aid," Reddric admits, after completing the circle.

"Ohh, how sinister."

"Okay, we're ready."

Having seen this ritual done many times in his adolescent, Aaron lies down inside the center circle, stretching out his extremities to create a human star.

Red pulls out several trinkets, keepsakes and charms to represent the five corners of the inverted pentagram—earth, air, fire, water and the soul.

"Couldn't you just play 'Let's Groove," by Earth, Wind and Fire backwards to get the very same effect?" Aaron mocks.

"Shh, no talking." Red starts to read from another book, which resembles a school textbook—glossy cover and all.

The Kool-Aid turns dark purple as it pulsates in response to the pagan words. Magical lines crawl from the outer circumference and inward toward Aaron. Each one bites onto his spirit, removing his control over his own body. Aaron feels like a pack of wolves are feasting on his flesh, bite by bite. He pictures himself swatting them away with a fly swatter, and just when he feels like it's the end...it is.

Aaron is fully back in control of himself. His body levitates from the inner circle as he rises back to his feet in a cool sort of way.

Red is speechless. It worked.

"That is new. I have to admit, that might be much better for my lower-back problems for getting up in the mornings," Aaron says, giving this witch thing a second chance.

"How do you feel?" Red asks, finding his words again.

"Like an action hero. When do I get to murder bad guys in bulk?"

Red notices Aaron's newly accentuated features, which appear to be more prominent than they were moments before—chin, nose ears, even his eyebrows are sharper.

Red tries to make a crack, to point out this discovery, when Aaron walks right up to him, presses his lips against Red's newer head and gives it a deep, passionate kiss.

Upon their lips touching, the extra head explodes into shimmering dust. Aaron obliterates the curse that has plagued Red for years.

"Woah," Red says, feeling more himself than he has in ages. "Thanks! That guy's been a pain in my neck for years."

"Sorry about that. I just felt it somehow."

"I knew you had it in you—the power to take whatever you want, from whomever you want. You're a real witch!" Red inspects the vacant hole in his shirt. "I guess it's time to go shopping."

"Just to be clear, I was helping a friend, not making a pass at you." Aaron leafs through his mother's spell book. "Nothing has changed. It's gibberish," Aaron says, thumbing through the book he still can't read.

"Just fake it. Sound out the words slowly and take your time. The words are mere recipes. The real power is in the ingredients, which is you."

"But, I clam up every time I have to do public reading. I must have a phobia or something."

"Here." Red pulls out a pill bottle from his pile of junk. "Take one of these. I use them all the time when I have to focus really hard on a big spell."

"What does it do?"

"It keeps your attention focused, and the rest of the world in the background. It's like Adderall if it made a deal with the devil to increase potency."

"Wait, did it?"

"Yes, deals with the devil were made. But rest assured, it's totally safe and F.D.A. approved."

"Wait, you're telling me that the Food and Drug Administration approved this stuff?"

"No, the Fantastical Devil Association did."

"That doesn't make me feel any better. Is that a real group or just a devil-worshiping fan club?" Aaron takes the bottle and brings it to his ear, giving it a good shake.

"Careful!"

"Sorry. What luck is it that you had this stuff with you?"

"It wasn't luck, I brought it in case I was wrong and had to...banish you, like a demon."

"What? You weren't positive this was going to work?" Flames ignite inside Aaron's eyes.

"I had my doubts..."

Aaron's fingers start to grow long and sharp, like needles. "Like a demon? Do you realize how bad it would be to have to spend eternity with those swoosh bags?!"

"I'm sorry, it was a risk. But that risk was without merit. Everything turned out fine," Red stammers, moving backwards.

"I suppose you're right. Let's ruin a witch's day," Aaron says, as the elongated ailments that manifested on him subside.

^^^

It takes more than a miracle, but the crowd somehow manages to take their assigned spots to witness the birth of a new era.

Aaron conceals his cross-dress with the clothes he showed up in, before making his way backstage.

Whoever was the event coordinator for the coronation didn't pull any stops. Poetry is read by fire breathers, devil dancers move gracefully to heavy metal music, even the elementary kids do a scene from their school play, "Phantom Ate the Opera."

Aaron looks down at the event program and realizes that his uncle goes on right before the sacrificial lamb. He feels sorry for the little chop, but if everything goes to plan, it may live through the ceremony.

Aaron's stomach lurches at the sight of Maliconious taking center stage. It is time, though Aaron's feet are glued to the stone floor, unable to move.

Maliconious is already speaking in an unfamiliar tongue as he holds up the ceremonial dagger. Next to him is a boiling cauldron with a stone lid, which is shaking and rattling from the scalding hot liquid inside. After a long display of hocus pocus, his uncle introduces Aaron and signals for him to join him, with an encouraging wave. His introduction is well received by the sound of one person clapping, who is most likely Reddric.

Aaron knows it is his time to shine, but his feet won't move an inch. All he can do is peek out at all the eager eyes awaiting his imminent failure. Sitting behind Reddric, Aaron spies the group of cultists. Thinking about each cultist bare-assed at the urinal gives him the strength to overcome his stage fright. With a bounce in his step and a hidden giggle behind his lips, he makes his way on stage.

Aaron thought that wearing the dress before was uncomfortable, but wearing it under another set of clothes makes it much worse. He walks as if he has a perpetual wedgie right past dozens of casters from all different sects—vamps, wares, and worse. He can feel their judgment as they ridicule, mock and whisper about him under their breath. He knows what they're thinking, "Is he going to pick that, or what?" Even the decorative cats seem to be laughing at him. He hates them in that moment as he makes his way to the sacrificial podium, only stopping briefly to pet the lamb with a noose around its neck.

Aaron stands beside his uncle who is quick to place the blade on the blood-scarred stone carving before taking his place between the children and fire breathers.

Aaron hesitates to pick up the cloudy dagger he was charged with cutting himself with. The blade is clearly made from salt, and the hilt has lemon etchings that leak acidic liquid out of them. *Not stingy, my tuchus,* he thinks to himself while he gives his uncle an evil gaze.

His glossophobia moistens his palms, as each watchful eye presses on his fears. Ignoring Red's warning, he shakes the pill bottle before opening it up. The audience falls silent as they watch him struggle to open the child-proof cap. It's the disaster they all predicted and prayed for, and the comedy doesn't disappoint their expectations. Their laughter shakes the chandelier in the center of the hall.

Aaron can feel their thoughts, they figure the bottle is some pain reducing substance. One person, on the right side of the room, thinks it is a stool softener, for god knows why.

Finally, Aaron's new-found nails rip the top of the bottle off, exposing the inside. Unfortunately, all his shaking has shattered the pills into shards, and he has no idea how big a single pill was. Aaron doesn't want to under-prescribe himself and decides to consume the whole bottle's worth. They taste like feet—Faramila's feet to be more exact. She does seem like the type of person who would do business with the devil. He glances at her in the audience and sees her eagerly petting her Scottish fold shawl.

Aaron raises the dagger, holding out his palm.

He tries to ignore the low chanting from his uncle behind him, "Cut...cut...cut..."

Keeping his eyes on Faramila, he brings the dagger down swiftly, using it to cut off his first layer of clothes, exposing his true self, dress and all. Aaron feels like a stage magician as he finishes his trick.

A choir of gasps fill the room.

"Shenanigans!" Faramila instantly tries to cast her aspersions among the crowd.

The dagger falls at his feet as he arms himself with something even more powerful—his mother's book of spells.

Before the shock of the event is fully assessed by the audience, Aaron starts to sound out words from his book of spells as the music erupts out of it, joining him in verse. His voice can barely be heard, even by himself, as he struggles to sound out the foreign language.

This isn't going to work. He isn't confident enough to pull off this caper. He will most likely spend the rest of his days as a witch's slave-boy, or worse—a window washer.

Suddenly, his body begins to tingle, and his voice booms as he gains pinpoint focus on the text. Nothing in the world exists except the symbols on the page. He reads each line to the best of his ability, "Kalamy roo, onless ocen e goo." Magical energy ignites off the pages of the sacred book.

One by one, the feline accessories start to hack up fur balls, which have eyes of their own and start to roll around. This seems quite peculiar to everyone, but not at all alarming. One of the furry-eyeball balls bites a spectating mummy's toe, and he lets out a howl.

Maliconious tries to interrupt his nephew, but a fire breather burps, engulfing him in flames.

Faramila knows this is not the work of a blessing spell crowning her as high priestess, but rather that of the evil arts. Aaron is up to something, and it isn't good for her or her ploy. She points and starts to yell to one of her disciples, "Do away with him at once!" Upon opening her mouth, an endless river of saliva pours out, making it nearly impossible for her to speak. Faramila's feline accessory hisses at the sight, despising water itself. The river of drool is drenching her clothes completely. Nobody liked her to begin with, but now they have a very wet reason to.

Maliconious leaps on top of her hoping she will put him out with her mouth.

Now, this is the train wreck they all want.

Unaware of the effects of his words, Aaron continues reading, as if in a trance, "Abbit ohli hati."

A ghoul wearing a top hat hears a nearby knocking sound. He looks around hoping someone else will get the door, wherever it is. The knocking continues, gradually getting faster and harder. A demon chick, wearing a pillbox hat, also hears the odd sound. Before long, everyone wearing a hat, headpiece or helmet is met with the same sensation. This consists of about one third of the audience. It seems that headgear is a fashion "yes" this year.

Everyone awkwardly smiles and shakes their heads, not knowing what to do, and not wanting to undo their whole outfit by removing the accessory. That is, until an invisible man takes off his cowboy hat, revealing a rabbit resting on his head. To everyone who is not an invisible entity, it appears to be suspended in midair.

Knowing that furry rodents always trump fashionable hats, each victim of the strange knocking looks under their cap or helm to find an adorable, fuzzy bunny of their own. Even Reddric is feeling jealous that he didn't wear a hat today.

This is fun, though a little distracting. No one is even noticing Aaron anymore. They are petting and playing with their newfound pets. It doesn't take long before there is an equal amount of fur-balls as attendees—some even have one in each arm. This is turning out to be the cutest witch ceremony to date.

Then, Faramila's feral stole pounces on a baby bunny and pandemonium ensues. The adorable scene turns quickly into an uproarious panic, as flashes of lop-eared fur hop every which way.

Most people think rabbits are docile, quiet, timid creatures. That is true, until the moment they release a lifetime of stored silence in one deafening scream. If you can imagine the effect of one of these creatures screeching, multiply that by a thousand, and that's the situation we're in right now. Every stained-glass window, dish, chandelier, glassware and potion in the building shatters into tiny shards. Even the small group of banshees are covering their ears in hope of escaping the cacophony.

If this hectic moment can't distract Aaron, nothing can. "Spina winton," Aaron continues on, fumbling through the words with an accent that could almost be described as racist towards witches and warlocks alike. The power of his mother flows through his veins, pumping magic energy through his heart and spells out of his lips. He is unknowingly accepting the role as high priestess, like it or not.

Red begins to fight his way through the flying rabbit/cat cyclone that starts to pick up. Everyone is getting scratched, kicked, and hissed at, as the disaster twists and churns anything that is smaller than a person into cat-agory bun tornado.

Bursting out of the kitchen comes the one-handed chef who is fencing a giant leech with a spatula. His grin encompasses most of his face, as he has finally found the fight he was trying to start with Aaron.

One of Faramila's slaves rushes over to her, holding her spell book on his back like a good little table. The page is already open to the chapter titled "Sudden Death and Daiquiris."

With Faramila's river of drool, and the cyclone knocking everyone off balance, it looks like an ice skating rink filled with toddlers—everyone is butthurt.

A group of what appear to be British moose are drinking tea and talking about the sudden change of weather. Red isn't sure if they are guests, conjured, or simply people transformed by Aaron. In any case, they are delightful to look at.

Liquid from broken potions mix together making new concoctions, which explode on impact.

Gravity is beginning to slip, as a hole is being torn leading to "The Void of Truth."

All the commotion awakens the vampire horde that were sound asleep in the crypt below. They barge into the room like starving college students invited to a free buffet.

The gust of wind from the animal twister lifts the robes of the dark cultists, answering Aaron's question about them wearing underpants or not. They do not.

Too bad he is too focused on his task to witness all the chaos for himself.

"Oilapunt so margoni," Aaron reads on with great fanfaronade.

At this point, Reddric is just fascinated with what will happen next. He scours the room as the chaos rages on, but he is unable to make out whatever "Oilapunt so margoni" is. It's just the same madness as before.

All the books in the room have joined the cats and other smaller objects in the cyclone, like an impractical washing machine on spin cycle.

A bible-belt cowboy, of all people, throws a lasso into the cyclone and manages to rope himself a spell book.

With crispy clothing, Maliconious rushes over to the cowboy and snatches the book out his rope. Something strange has happened to this book. It is flapping like a bird, trying to escape his grasp. Under further inspection, Maliconious realizes that it has been transformed from a "spell book" into a flying "smell book," and it is now a dirty diaper posing as a tome.

He looks to the cowboy for something to wipe his hands on, and he is met with a very polite "take one step closer to me and I'll hog tie you" kind of expression.

It is then that the Lemon Blade is hurled through the air and stabs Maliconious right in the shoulder (incidentally, in the right shoulder). "It stings! It stings so very much!" he cries out in pain.

The vampires are moving through the room, draining victim after victim, until another spell flies out of Aaron's mouth. Suddenly, they no longer crave blood. Now they want soy lattes and are self-righteous. It appears that Aaron has turned all the vampires into vegans.

Someone manages to open the outer doors, and the cyclone is quick to make a break for it—onward to the closest trailer park, or Florida. Following the twister is a stampede of guests who desperately want their fluffy-bun-puff-tails back.

Faramila crawls toward Aaron, holding her mouth closed. Hate fills her eyes as she makes her way up the stone stairs leading to the stage.

Red spies and tries to intercept her, but an animated tree reaches out its largest branch and swipes at him. He pauses, noticing two bunny rabbits gnawing on its roots. "Awww," he and the tree say in unison. Red is always distracted by cuteness and cat videos.

Faramila rips the book out of Aarons hands, ending the trance he was in.

He looks around in amazement at the chaos he has created. "Did I...I..."

He can hear Faramila's infuriation radiating outward from her eyes, *You contumacious man-child!* All his power has been stolen out of his hands, and the extent of his actions is starting to sink in. Swirling magical dust springs from her fingertips as she uses sign language to cast a spell of her own.

Aaron winces as he awaits his impending doom. He has failed his mother once again, and this time it was far worse than the time taped over her soap opera with cartoons.

Before she can finish casting, the caldron lid opens just long enough for a giant hand to come out and grab her. It pulls her into the boiling pot, melting her flesh right off her body. Aaron hates to admit it to himself, but it smells good.

Aghast, Red finally reaches his friend, who is licking his lips. "Aaron! Aaron! You did it!"

A loud burp bubbles out of the caldron.

"It's over. It's over!" Red says, hardly able to contain his excitement.

"Did we win?"

"I would say we did."

Pieces of the ceiling are falling sporadically. This ancient cathedral has lasted over two thousand years under generation after generation of spell casters, yet it only took a mere ten minutes for Aaron to destroy it.

"You knew that if I read from her book, I would assume her role, didn't you?" Aaron asks.

"What do I know? I'm just a warlock," Red says with a suspicious smile.

"You tricked me."

"I prefer the term 'outwit.'"

Aaron grabs the rope leash on his new pet lamb and causally makes his way toward the exit. "I'm taking this."

He gives one final glance to his uncle, who is making the same sound a soda can makes when you let out the carbonation slowly while he struggles with removing the Lemon Blade.

Stepping over the wreckage, corpses, and a teenage couple making out, they make their way out of the grand room. Red looks up at the fine art pieces lining the Corridor of Destiny.

"Oilapunt so margoni," he says, noticing that each portrait was changed into macaroni and paste style art. "Nicely done, I would have never guessed," Red says.

"I've always appreciated children's art," Aaron admits with a laugh.

"What are you going to do now, high priestess?" Red asks, as they exit the building, looking outward at the millions of white lights covering every surface of the outside world.

"I feel like dancing," Aaron says excitedly, as he gazes up at the moon, which he has turned into the largest disco ball in existence.

A smile forms on both their faces that won't leave for a very long time.

The End

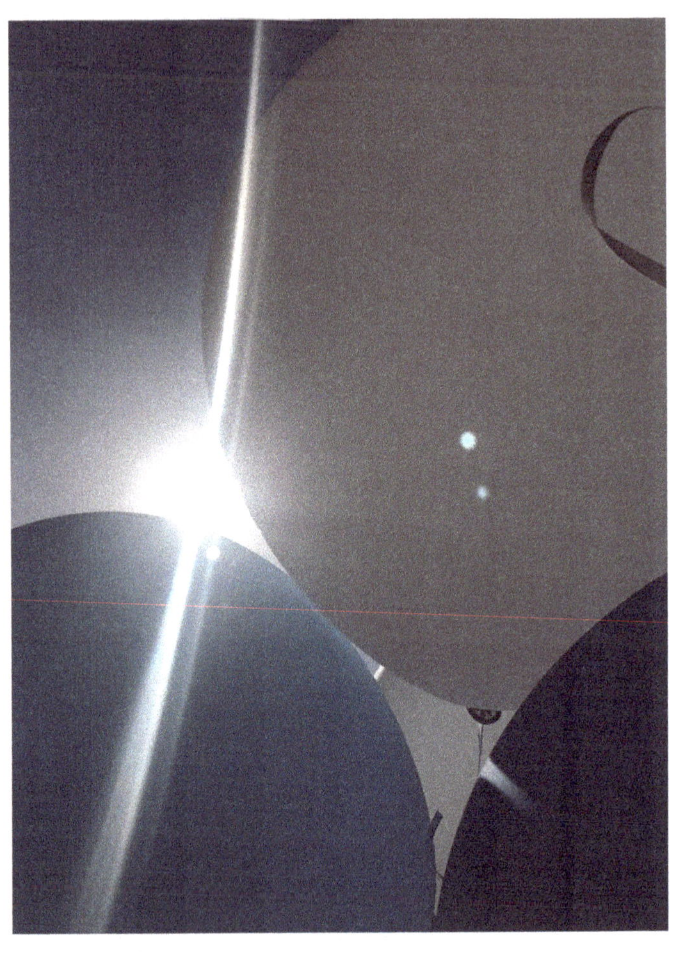

# HERE WE GO AGAIN

Caught on a line, hungry for the truth

I starved myself for so long, I forgot how to hurt

From the rubber band snap, I feel an emotional sting

I always try to flee, but run back into the scene

The skeletons in my closet were buried by a dog

I'm scratching at the ground, looking to grave rob

Why can't I bleed without making a sound?

Never find the words to make me profound

Like an accident you can never take back

It always helps to love, to have a heart attack

# OBSOLETE

It's quite handy sending work through a smart phone.

Image sent.

Jim reflects on a time far less fortunate, involving fax machines, laser discs and typewriters, as he sifts through old boxes in the garage.

Jim is always up to date with the latest technology. He had a compact disc player before they were called "CDs," he bought a new car because it came with a car phone, and he would get a new pager every six months during their heyday. He wants the best, and he wants to have it first.

Through years of gadgets and gismos, Jim got a reputation for being hip to the newest fads. His critical views and reviews became famous within the ever-expanding tech world. Big-name companies send him beta and concept devices for his perusing fingers.

Never one for throwing things away, Jim's garage soon became a complete history of the consumer doohickeys. It resembles a museum of obsolete artifacts. He only uses each contraption long enough for a newer model to come and replace it, leaving most of this junk in near-mint condition.

Jim has been commissioned to write an article about the best mobile phone of all time. This is a tough assignment because out of every whatchamacallit and thingamabob he has accumulated over the years, phones were what he had acquired the most of—primarily due to so many companies jumping on the cellular bandwagon, releasing multiple models in several series each year. He has flip phones, phones with keyboards, even thick ones with telescopic antennas.

He moves past his tower of answering machines, steps through a labyrinth of printers, scanners and copy machines, and squeezes between his stacks of personal robots from the '80s. He finally makes it to the great wall of mobiles. It isn't a wall, really—it is a large bookshelf spanning the length of one whole wall with banker boxes sorted by year. Even though it was only March, this year's box was almost full.

One by one, he pulls the boxes off the shelves and brings them into his den. Removing one box uncovers a hidden one behind. Before this, Jim hadn't realized exactly how many he truly has and how long he has been collecting them.

After a while, he has moved the last piece of furniture out of his den necessary to accommodate the vast amount of cell phones and accessories. His ivory chess set, a wooden globe set atop a pedestal, and his advanced massaging armchair are a few notable mentions that are ousted from the once delightfully cozy leisure room.

Jim carefully arranges the dust-ridden boxes around himself, leaving no clear escape route in case of an emergency. He must finish his task before he can get on with his social media or any other day-to-day distractions. Sitting cross-legged in the center of the ring of boxes, he rubs his hands together in excitement, creating heat from the friction. "Here we go!"

Next to him is a strategically placed power strip with ten available outlets for his top ten picks. First, he starts his vetting process with the oldest year, picking one phone to represent that era. Once he makes his selection, he places it on top of the box with all its whatsits. He continues in this fashion with each box.

Now he is faced with the harder task of whittling it down to ten, knowing this is the criteria for the article. Taking a second pass, he carefully looks at each finalist's buttons, stability, and briefly thumbs through its manual to corroborate its features against his memory of them. This proves to be a much more difficult culling process.

There's a clear pattern he starts to recognize. He notices that while newer phones may have sleeker designs, they lack features of their older counterparts.

Nearing the stroke of midnight, he finds the "magnificent ten" and the title for his article.

As the phones charge, Jim powers each one on. The start-up sounds bring him back to his past, almost like a time machine. Each handheld device is a time capsule dedicated to a precise moment in his life. Giddy with excitement, he takes a trip on memory express.

Each one feels like an old photo album of ex-girlfriends. So many goodtime memories overwhelm him as a genuine smile grows on his face.

One of his choices holds evidence of a time when he was obsessed with comic books. It was the first of its kind to offer ink-realism to the screen, a feature that has been refined many times since. Jim had gone a little overboard with testing this feature by filling up the memory with rare graphic stories.

After finishing one of his old favorites, he stops himself from reading the next in the series. He must avoid letting the rest of the night get away from him. "I don't have time for this," he says to himself, hoping that saying it aloud will help him comply with his own order.

Jim reads texts from friends he has long forgotten, scrolls through pictures of places he never remembers going to, and reviews contacts he never recalls making acquaintance with. It's a blissful moment for him that is short-lived. He realizes that not only did he upgrade his devices, he also upgraded his life. So many contacts are lost in this ancient technology, so much of himself.

He starts to copy some old contacts that had been lost, without having any real intention of contacting any of them for drinks. Still, Jim feels closer to them knowing they're only one click away.

The Saber alone has more than three times the contacts of his current phone. It is also the oldest of the lot. At the time, it was touted as having an excellent camera. As he browses the stored pictures, there is no debate—it is truly magnificent. Though the standard phones of today have far surpassed it in pixel count alone, there is something about that camera. Each image has a yellowish haze, as though it were from the '70s. It reminds him of a time when photographers used to put Vaseline on the lens to lessen the image's detail.

That's the problem with the super-high definition of today; you see every imperfection, every blemish and every stroke of the makeup brush. Nothing hides from the digital eye. Until, of course, you process the hell out of it through your airbrush app—making your selfie look perfect, though somewhat inhuman. Vanity knows no bounds with filter and overlay effects.

There's something beautiful and real about this forgotten treasure. The Saber is nearly sixteen years old, yet it's still as solid as a rock. The slide-out keyboard fits great in his palm. There are no auto-correct issues with this one. He starts to type out his rave review of the thing, forgetting how fast he can type two-handed. No wonder he found a bunch of poetry stored in its memory.

What the Saber lacks in technology, it more than makes up for in versatility. It has many features that phones today make you pay for. One example is the ability to record your own ringtone. If he wanted a song, he just recorded, cut and saved it within minutes. He finds many custom-made tones he had created back in the day.

"The phone is riiiiingiiiing. Pick me uuuuuup. Stop playing gaaaaaames. You're so lameeees," his much younger voice sings as he browses the ringtones.

He can't help but let out a chuckle, as he remembers how he used to franticly try and answer incoming calls before the last line played out. It is this sort of naivety that he used to attribute to his youth. Before the reviews, promotions and respect of his peers, life used to be simple and fun.

The Saber even came with its own AM/FM radio player where you could record live broadcasts onto MP3.

Fingers frantic, he can't stop playing with the contraption long enough to take notes. Feeling very attached to this device, he knows it needs to be the "best in show," even despite its age. Jim contemplates reactivating it, though he knows it has long since been made obsolete. New networks will never allow its 32-bit processing and what have you.

Cycling through the low-fidelity pictures, he notices a woman he hasn't thought about for a very long time. It is Stacy, or Ace for short. She had defiant hair that fought against gravity, and a contagious sort of smile.

Jim can't remember exactly why they broke up, but he does recall it was around the time he upgraded from the Saber. Come to think of it, that must have been the reason he stopped using the cell in the first place. He had needed a fresh start.

He can't remember them ever having a bad time together, and the pictures only convince him further of this. Was she the love of his life?

He wonders what might have happened if he had never upgraded his life as he looks through the old text messages between them. Would he still be single today?

Stacy: "Did you see the mustache on that guy last night?"

Jim: "Yes! It looked as though that 'stash was wearing him."

Stacy: "You should get one of those. Then maybe I might fall in love with you <3"

Jim: "You mean you haven't already? I'm shocked, bewildered...impressed!"

Stacy: "Look, a girl must keep to her father's standards for a suitor."

Jim: "I've met your dad. I don't think facial hair is one of them."

Stacy: "Not just any facial hair, the longest in the land. Only the manliest of males, and the toughest of tigers will be enough for my dear old dad."

Jim: "I tried to grow a beard once. Only thing is, when I slept, a kitten licked it off."

Stacy: "Must be your milky-white complexion. You should try getting outside more often."

Jim: "I only wish I weren't joking ;)"

Stacy: "Well, that's certainty cute, in your own sort of way."

Jim: "So, you think I'm cute, do you?"

Stacy: “I love that you’re cute ^_^”

Jim: “So, you do love me?”

Stacy: “If I am going to start saying stuff like that, it’s going to be in person, followed by a kiss. :-* LYMTW.”

Jim: “What does that mean?”

Stacy: “I’ll have to show you :P”

Jim: “Tomorrow then?”

Stacy: “--`--,--`{@”

As Jim reaches the end of the text thread, tears fill his eyes. He doesn’t remember anything of significance from the following day, or what LYMTW meant. How could he forget such a meaningful conversation, such a joyous time in his life?

Ace was a florist by trade, and he finds hundreds of pictures of wildflowers he had captured for her. Each one tells its own beautiful story. Jim wonders why he ever stopped his artistic ventures. The answer is clear—he was no longer inspired to reflect his emotions. As he upgraded devices, he also unknowingly upgraded other aspects of himself, and some features no longer seemed relevant anymore.

Before he knows it, he is taking a picture of a flower image right off the Saber’s screen. This goes on through the wee hours of the night, taking pictures of pictures to savor the feelings they unearth deep inside himself. Without thinking it through, he adds Ace’s old number to his current phone.

The sun comes up around the time he snaps the last photo. It is of a rose with perfectly spherical water droplets covering its rich petals, from a recent rain. Exhausted, Jim curls up on the ground with his archaic phones surrounding him like a ring of protection. He dreams of Ace and their moments together.

***

Jim awakens with purpose, never thinking about how much of himself is buried, so much of himself left inside this screen. Before taking to his morning routine, he scrolls through the photos again. They incite just as much emotion as they had the previous night. Before he can change his mind, he starts to text Ace.

*This is insane, no one keeps the same number for sixteen years*, he thinks to himself as he deletes his text. Then he thinks about fate. *What is the harm in trying?* Worst case scenario, the person at the other end tells him it's a wrong number, and he can move on. Thinking of her gives him a happy feeling in the pit of his stomach. He knows that he has to do it.

"One text. And if it's not her, you're going to drop this whole thing and finish the article." He needs to set a limit for himself, so that things won't get out of control. He can see himself getting caught up in the moment and hiring a private investigator, or doing one of those internet records searches. He doesn't want to go that deep and become some deranged stalker. One text is all he is committing to, and one text is all he will send.

Jim: ~~"I bet you never expected to hear from me again."~~

Jim: ~~"You never told me what LYMTW meant."~~

Jim: ~~"Are you still alive?"~~

Jim: "Hi. Remember me?" he types out, lingering over the send button. Is he ready for this? To open a whole world he had long since forgotten. Before he can erase his text for a fourth time, he sends the thing.

"One text," he utters under his breath, staring at the phone while it sends. Ten minutes of looking at a blank screen feels like an hour. Finally, he gets a notification that the message has been read!

He waits and waits, with no reply.

He is obsessing over it and debates sending a follow-up apology forgetting the whole thing, but he refrains. "Don't give up now, not like you did in the past," he tells himself.

The waiting is killing him. His deadline is approaching fast, and he hasn't even written one word of the article.

Breakfast has long since passed, and now it is a couple hours after lunch. He ought to stop fixating on the screen before his battery goes completely dead.

Knowing his texts forward automatically to his watch, computer and tablet, he decides to make some food, to take his mind off things.

The want of his hunger is bigger than the size of his mouth, as he stacks meat inside a simple sandwich. Bread, meat, mayo and a pickle, that's all he needs. None of those other ingredients to distract from the real stuff he desires. Struggling to fit his mouth around the sandwich, he notices a notification on the display of his refrigerator. Spilling deli ham on the floor, he rushes to the appliance.

Bells chime and lights flicker throughout his house from all the other contrivances that are paired to his phone. His slippery mayonnaise fingers reach for the digital light controller on the fridge's display.

Dimming the overhead lights turns his living room/kitchen into a magical display of flashing LEDs and notification sounds. This beautifully orchestrated dance is only surpassed by department store Christmas displays. He ponders how he must look to outsiders. His tech lifestyle has been running him, and he is more connected to his machines than to real people in real life.

He pauses, only briefly, to look at himself and life from a different perspective. Before reading the text notification, he takes a moment to finish his sandwich and revel in its artistry.

After washing his hands, he decides to undo the unrest that he has created inside the den.

Now everything is back to normal, except the magnificent ten, which are now proudly displayed on his coffee table. He is merely keeping himself preoccupied to avoid reading the response. *What if it changes my life somehow? What will I do?*

His only saving grace is that he doesn't feel at all inspired to write his piece. He walks over to his living room cuckoo clock and presses a button. The wheels and cogs spin until the little wooden saloon doors swing wide open and a fuzzy bird staggers out.

"Cheep. New message from Ace. 'Who is this?' Cheep, cheep," the bird reads the notification before spinning around and heading back from where it came.

The sound of Jim's lips smacking shows his disappointment in the response. There's nothing to fear—no rejection, only a forgotten friend.

Jim retrieves his phone from its wireless charging station, contemplating his response.

Jim: "I know it has been a long time. I came across this, and I wanted to share it." He attaches his favorite of the flower pictures that he took.

Ace: "I deleted your number for good reason."

He wipes the perspiration off his forehead.

Jim: "I know. I'll leave you alone now."

"There you have it. She hates me. Why does she hate me? I don't remember us ever fighting. She got busy with work...I do remember that, but that's it."

Jim tosses his phone on the table, kicking his feet up next to it. "I tried. No harm done. I didn't want anything more than that anyway." Jim leans his head back, holding his neck, thinking about his article—at least trying to think about it.

A new notification rings throughout the house. Still in the dark, Jim scrambles to reach his phone, falling over himself and collapsing on the floor.

He loses time.

Taking in a deep breath through his nose, he admires the fragrance of his thick carpet. "That's nice."

Remembering the message, Jim crawls to the coffee table like a zombie climbing out of a shallow grave.

He finally reconnects with his phone again. Ace has sent him two messages.

Ace: "That's really beautiful."

Ace: "Where did you find that?"

Jim contemplates responding. He had already exceeded his one text limit.

*It would be rude if I didn't... What time did she send those texts? I feel so relaxed and well rested...*

While entrenched in thought, his fingers hammer out a response and send it away.

Jim: "I took it while thinking of you."

He can't believe his eyes. "What the...no. Why did I write that?" Not that it was exactly untrue, but far too blunt for a first contact—especially after sixteen years.

Again, he's back to staring at his phone, reading the whole thread out loud to himself. He has texting remorse and thinks of dozens of more appropriate responses.

Feeling embarrassed, he powers down his phone. "Digging up the past is digging your own grave," he says, reaching for his tablet to start his work on.

No sooner does he write out the title, "The Magnificent Ten," than a message from Ace overlays his page.

Ace: "I've missed you."

"Damn it," he blurts out.

He ponders how he can't even get away from technology for one minute. He has issues, he now realizes, as if this whole venture has been an unknowing intervention he is putting upon himself.

This time he thinks a lot about his response. He has no idea what he is getting involved with by texting her. It has been a very long time, and a lot could have changed within that time. *Is she divorced? Did she let herself go?*

Not that jumping back into things where they left off is even an option. God knows, he didn't exactly become something ideal for her, or anyone, for that matter. Sixteen years ago, he had all the potential at his fingertips, and now all he can show for that time spent are these machines. Sure, he lived comfortably, in a nice neighborhood, but he rarely went outside to enjoy it. Probably because he had no one to enjoy it with.

He takes dozens of selfies, hoping that if he sends her one, she might do the same. The only problem is, he cannot find one that is at all flattering. Nothing comes close to measuring up to the flower he sent her that the Saber had taken. Thinking that contraptions are what got him into this mess, he gives up on the whole selfie idea.

Jim: "I want to see you. Will you meet me?"

Before receiving a response, he is already scouring the internet for a local café for them to meet at. If his memory serves him correctly, Stacy always liked to drink Italian soda with cream.

Ace: "I promised myself I wouldn't."

Jim: "I understand."

He wonders why he ever reached into the past. There is always a reason for leaving people there. He pulls his arm back, ready to give into his disappointment and throw his phone against the wall. Just then, it alerts him, almost like a cry for mercy. He looks down at it, gripping it tightly.

Ace: "But I will see you. Just this once."

Thinking about how fast his state-of-the-art phone receives messages, he kisses it before responding.

Jim: "How about this place?" He attaches a link to a five-star café that looks both quaint and romantic.

Ace: "That place is a little far for me. How about this one?" she counters, sharing a link of her own.

Jim inspects her 3-star choice over his. It looks cheap and has more negative reviews than positive. One review states that a customer got food poisoning there three times. Jim wonders what kind of person goes back after one incident of food poisoning, let alone two. He also reflects upon what kind of person goes to a place after reading such a horrendous review. The answer is apparent—he is that kind of person.

Jim: "Meet you there in an hour?"

Ace: "Okay, I'll start walking over in a bit."

*Walking? She was always into hikes and nature. Maybe that means she lives close by. Of course, that's what that means.* Jim snaps out of his inner thoughts as he realizes that he has only an hour.

A shower, shave, self-inflicted hair trimming, and three outfits later, he's on his way to meet "the one that got away"—or at least, the one he let get away.

After a short drive, he pulls up to the run-down establishment and instantly knows that this is not the sort of place to rekindle anything, unless it is insurance fraud.

Jim glances at his smart watch, seeing that he is perfectly on time, as usual. Ace was always early, if he remembers her correctly. She was the only person who made him feel tardy even when he wasn't. Giving himself one final glance in the reflection of his fully loaded car, he straightens out his attire.

*Am I really going through with this?*

He takes in a deep breath and holds it while making his way to the little taco hut. Jim mistakenly barges into the kitchen, thinking there's more to the establishment.

He catches an older lady off-guard. A black hairnet covering her aged hair, she has on a large, flowery dress and impractical, black high heels. "Out! Get out of here!"

Jim is instantly shooed out of the kitchen, as if he had walked in on someone using the toilet. He finally starts breathing normally as he stumbles through the correct entrance.

Looking around at the patrons for Stacy, he can't help but wonder how she would look now. Unfortunately, no one his age is sitting alone. Not wanting to take up a seat without being a customer, he orders a single taco from the agitated lady he barged in on a moment ago, this time from the right side of the counter.

"Do you accept phone payments?" he asks, holding up his device which has plenty of credit stored on it.

She gives him a peculiar look, as if he is speaking another language entirely. It wasn't English or Spanish, it was tech talk, and no, she didn't speak it.

He pulls out a ten-dollar bill that has been inside his wallet for maybe a year now. Before she can finish ringing him up, he refuses his change, letting it be her tip. He takes the tiny sombrero with his order number on it and occupies an empty table, glancing at his watch—fourteen after.

It wasn't like Ace to be tardy. Many unlikely scenarios plague his mind, each coming from his own insecurities.

His taco arrives the same time he gets a message. The server may as well have been invisible at that moment, as he watches Jim whip out his phone like a ravenous dog.

Ace: "Are you coming? Or is this another one of your silly games?"

Jim visibly hedges from the message, instantly looking around for her. Nope, she is certainly not here. He double-checks the location she sent him, and there's no doubt about it, he is at the right place. Using technology to his advantage, he "checks in" to his location, marking his GPS position on the global map and pinging her with the pinpoint coordinates.

Like a cat watching a moth, he intently studies everyone eating their food in the outdoor seating area. A young woman with a single taco on her plate suddenly picks up her phone. She looks up, directly at Jim, almost terrified.

That is her...but she is definitely *not* Stacy.

She silently curses to herself and abruptly gets up from her seat, quickly grabbing her taco.

Thinking about how he must look—like some internet predator preying on young girls; she looks so scared—he feels horrible about what he might have done. He stands up and proceeds to follow her.

"Sir, sir! Your food?" the server yells at Jim's back, as Jim trails the girl.

Never taking his eyes off her, Jim quickly returns to the table and grabs the tinfoil-wrapped taco. Almost skipping, he spots the young woman exiting the parking lot.

"Hey, wait," he yells, hoping to ease her mind. Instead, it forces her to move even faster.

Knowing he's only made things worse, he gets into his car and drives after her in an attempt to reassure her, never thinking for a moment that it would further make him look the part of kidnapper or human trafficker. Hanging half his body out of the driver-side window, he follows her down the next street.

She cautiously looks over her shoulder at the fast-approaching car. "Stop following me," she screams, turning her head forward.

"I need to talk to you for a minute."

"I thought you were someone else. Sorry for the mix-up," she says, holding up her hands in disgust.

"I just want to let you know that I am *not* a rapist."

She stops and looks directly at him this time. "I never thought you were until you said that just now!" Rummaging through her purse, she drops her to-go taco.

Getting a closer look at the girl, he figures out that she is a minor. Now he fears that he most certainly is going to jail if he doesn't handle this correctly.

Pulling out a larger-than-normal can of pepper spray, she aims it directly at him.

Jim watches internet videos, and he's seen a ton that involve unsuspecting victims of that stuff. He proceeds to roll up his windows before she can douse him with the canned irritant. Brownish liquid coats his glass as the pungent smell of pepper wafts in through his A/C vents. Coughing and hacking, he turns off the car, hoping to stop the vent from flowing. Pawing around as if he no longer has opposable thumbs, Jim climbs over to the passenger-side door and rolls out, gasping for fresh air.

"Where do you think you're going?" the girl asks, bounding around to his side of the car, while letting her anger distort her face.

Holding his hands up, Jim begins to rise to his feet. "I...don't want to hurt you." The constant dinging of his ajar door agitates him almost as much as the fumes emanating from the other side.

She doesn't believe him and lets loose her finger against the trigger of the can. It lets out a sad little sound, but no liquid comes out. It sounds almost like a fart you try and pass off as your chair. She must have used it all on the car.

"Can I just...do this?" Jim closes the door, stopping the dreadful dinging sound.

"I'm *not* getting in your car, freak!" She shakes the can and tries once more—still nothing.

"Look, I just want to talk to you. Here, to prove it..." Jim throws his keys off into the distance. Unfortunately, never being that athletic, they land inside a spiky bush.

"That doesn't change anything. You could have a white van stashed around here...somewhere." She looks around suspiciously. "Who are you? How did you get my number?"

"It was stored inside an old phone I had. I also thought you were someone else."

"Who did you think I was?" she asks, now holding the pepper spray high above her head, as if she is seriously considering throwing it at him.

"Ace. My ex-girlfriend." Saying it out loud makes Jim realize how much Stacy had meant to him. She was more than just an ex, she was *the* ex.

"I'm obviously not that guy! So, can you leave me alone now?"

"Ace is a woman, not a boy. But, that doesn't matter anymore."

"Then why are you chasing me?"

"I didn't want you to think I was a creep."

The girl lowers her can to ponder what he said. "You know, trying to run someone over with your car is a lot worse than having a wrong number!"

"I wasn't trying to run...ugh...look, do you mind telling me why you agreed to meet?" Jim asks, leaning his back against the door in a non-threatening way.

"If I answer, you leave me alone, okay?"

Putting his hand on his forehead in frustration, Jim nods in agreement.

"I also thought you were my ex," the girl can't say without rolling her eyes. "Brock is his name. We dated a long time...almost two months."

"In my experience, anyone named Brock is a total tool."

The girl lets out a laugh and leans up against the back bumper of the car casually. "It was the picture you sent. I thought Brock had really changed, finally started to respect me, but I guess I was wrong."

"I'm sorry to hear that. You're a pretty girl. I'm sure you deserve better," Jim says, causing her to stand upright with a scowl. "Not that it's me! I date people my own age. Really, I do!"

"So, why chase me down like a lunatic? I almost called the cops on you."

"Honestly, it was those pictures. I was trying to reach out to the person who inspired me to take pictures like that. The thing is, the phone is quite old, and I should've known that she moved on long ago."

"You mean there are more?" the girl says, taking a step closer.

"Sure. You want to see?" Jim pulls out his phone, which catches her fancy.

She hesitates before leaning in, making sure he sees her closed fist. "Is that..."

"Sure is."

"I thought it wasn't due out until summer," she says, pulling it out of his hands for further inspection. "Are you sure this thing is real?"

"It is. I'm reviewing it for a blog I host." He holds out his open palm, offering to unlock it.

She places it inside his hand, trying to hide her excitement.

Holding the screen to his eye, she watches in amazement as it does a retinal scan to unlock. "This is only one of the many new features it has."

"Lucky. That's so cool."

"It is pretty neat. I'm not a huge fan of the camera, though." Jim hands her back the phone, with another flower image displayed on the screen. He watches her reaction as she scrolls through his masterpieces. So many emotions develop on her face, each one rich and radiant.

"These are spectacular. You really must have loved this Ace person."

"I think I did. I just never told her."

"Is that why you sent me that text, to tell her?"

"Maybe. I wasn't sure exactly what I was going to say until I said it. There was this one thing she told me once, and I wanted closure, I think."

"Really? What did she say?" the teen asks, never prying her eyes from the images.

"That's the thing, I don't know. All she said was 'LYMTW.'"

"Love You More Than Words," the girl says without hesitation.

"What?"

"LYMTW. My mother used to say that to me all the time when I was little."

"Where did you say you got that phone from?" Jim asks, wondering how long ago Ace moved on.

"My mother." The girl looks up at him differently, as she starts to connect the dots. "I gotta go." She tosses the phone at him, and he fumbles to keep it from falling on the ground.

She's already twenty feet away by the time he stops bobbling the contraption.

Jim thinks it's strange for her to leave so abruptly. Then he too finishes piecing it together.

First, he rushes to the bush where he tossed his keys. Knowing this is a lost cause, he starts to chase her down by foot. "Wait. Hold on! You know something."

"Leave me alone!" she yells, matching his pace, leaving no room for him to catch up.

She's much younger and more fit. Jim knows he cannot keep up with her forever. "Stacy is her name. I knew your mother, didn't I?"

Nothing he said slowed her stride.

"Did I figure it out? Can you stop and talk to me for one second?"

This catches her attention. She turns around, tears streaking her young cheeks. This is exactly what Jim didn't want to happen.

"What did you think? We could have some father-daughter relationship now? By you tricking me, of all things? Huh, James?"

"What?" Jim wonders what she is talking about, and how she knows his name.

"How old would you say I am?"

His body collapses to the ground. He is focusing on her words more than on his wobbly legs. *Her father? I can't be. Stacy was never pregnant with my child.* He can't breathe, though he ignores it. *Is that what she wanted to talk to me about? Wait, Ace broke up with me. Maybe that's when she found out about the baby. Yes, that makes perfect sense. I remember her attitude changing. And I just let it happen, never asking her to reconsider.*

"James! Breathe!" the girl yells, propping up his bluish head.

Looking at her face calms him. He starts to see the resemblance. She has his nose and his hair color. Everything else is clearly from Ace.

"You look just like her. I don't know...how I never saw it until now."

"You mean, she never told you about me?"

"Of course not. Why would I be here...if I had known." Catching his breath, the girl lets go of his head, as if disgusted by touching him.

"Before you leave, just answer me one last thing."

With her arms folded together and sulking, she gives him a shrug.

"What's your name?"

"Janis," she says, shuffling her feet as she parts ways with him.

"Nice to meet...wait!"

"You said one last thing, lying bastard."

Jim bounds to his feet and approaches her, reaching out his phone.

She pushes it back to him, "I don't need or want anything from you."

"Just wait a minute." Jim uses his years of gadgeteering to quickly mess with his preferences using both his voice and fingers. "Phone, create new profile—Janis." Never has he worked so diligently and purposefully. "Delete all contacts except home number."

"What are you doing?" Janis asks with a sigh."

"The right thing."

"Task complete," the phone says.

"Almost done...Phone, what is the maximum credit allowance on this device?"

"Credits cannot exceed the amount of three thousand US dollars," the phone responds.

"Add maximum amount." A progress bar starts to fill up as the dollar amount grows.

"I cannot be bought like some prostitute!" Janis scoffs.

"I know. It's just a start," Jim says, handing her the proposed gift.

She reluctantly accepts his offering.

"I hope I can offer you something more in the future...if you'll let me," Jim says, a sense of pride and dignity quickening his words.

"Like what?"

"Fatherhood."

A softness returns to her face. "No, I can't accept this. It's too much. Besides, what are you going to use?"

"Something far better."

"What could possibly be better than this phone? It isn't even out yet."

"It's called...the Saber," Jim says, the thrill of youth returning to his eyes.

The End

## FORGOTTEN FLOWER

I surrender, gaining nothing in return
You start the fire, yet I feel the burn

If I only had a clue

I wish I never took my own advice
When I cut myself out of my own heist

Can you pay the bailiff for my crimes

Insomnia made me give up on my dreams
Like an unfaithful man hiding his wedding ring

A promise is a word that's never untrue

Just because someone treats you like garbage
don't think you're any less pretty or priceless

I am not the dirt underneath my feet

You open yourself up for the world to see
But they cut off your legs and leave you to bleed

Bought and sold to brighten a day

Like a flower in a trash can, that still smells sweet
You wait for a strange man to sweep you off your feet

...

# OUT OF MY MIND

Am I even alive? Darkness is all I know. I'm numb to the world around me, if one even exists. My thoughts are the only proof that I'm something.

*Objects can't think...can they?*

I cannot stop the emptiness from expanding. There has to be more than this silent torture.

*Still alone.*

This must be the place where time comes to die. How long has it been here? How long will it continue to be here? If this truly is nothingness, why am I here to witness it? If you can hear me, make it all go away. My anguish is everlasting. This has to be either the start of existence, or the end.

I want to scream for change; I want a lot of things.

Waiting...

I sense something different, and it gives me hope I'm not isolated—a smell, fresh and clean like metal. I'm not going crazy. There is more to this than waiting. More to me. It's getting stronger.

Something else is here—a beeping noise.

Sounds, I remember those.

I embrace its annoying tone. Life is being created around me. The beeping gets louder as it increases speed slightly.

My prayers are being answered. I feel as if I'm inside out, imploding into another state of existence. I don't like this feeling. I don't like any of it at all.

Snip. Snip. Snip.

I hear liquid spitting after each cut as I internally cringe. I hear something else. It's high pitched and mechanical. It reminds me of a tiny wheel.

It's getting closer.

I feel a breeze against me. Air...I *am* alive—a trace of existence existing.

PAIN!

So much pain. It won't stop. I want to go back to nothingness. I can't move. I can't stop it. Why do I feel it? It's going to kill me.

My eyes open wide.

A surgeon jerks his hand away from my head; red liquid sprays everywhere. It's in my eye, on his latex glove. He is holding a bloody, circular saw. It's my blood. Why is he cutting me?

"Nurse, come look at this," the doctor says, pulling away from me.

A masked woman looks closely into my eyes, shining a light in each one. "They're dilated," she says.

"I'm more concerned that they're open." He drops the saw on an instrument tray and pulls off his gloves, turning them into each other. "Fix it."

While making his exit, he tosses the balled-up gloves into a bio hazard bin. He clenches his fist after making the shot.

The nurse mixes a brown liquid into a clear vial, shaking it up violently. She attaches a large needle to the vial and positions it to my eye. The point looks enormous as it approaches. A drop of the liquid is resting on the tip.

"This will only hurt a lot," she says with a smirk.

The sharp point starts to go into my socket. Inside, I feel the smallest of movements from her hand. Even her pulse causes pain to shoot through my skull.

Be still, be still.

Her fingers are poised to inject the brown liquid into me.

Is that stuff going to make me better, or worse?

I want this all to end.

I blink.

Frightened, she pulls the needle out of my eye, dropping it on the ground. "Shoot," she says retrieving it, only now the pointy bit is bent.

She's coming back for another pass. She didn't sterilize it after it fell. That's not right. Clearly, she cares little for her job, and nothing for me.

The end of the needle is about to enter me again; I see debris sticking to the tip. The nurse hesitates, pulling it back to her. She tries to bend it back into place. Her hand slips and she gets stabbed right through her glove, the thin latex shredding, exposing her bloodied palm.

She rushes out of the room, wrapping her wound up in the end of her scrubs, applying pressure.

My eyes squint from the overhead light.

I have movement.

I can move my eyes around; I can see things. On the wall, there's an educational poster about the brain. This is a hospital, and I'm a patient. Am I sick? I see an X-ray film on a screen. It shows a full body scan with multiple notes written in white. There's a name; I can almost make it out.

It says "Andrew."

That must be me. I'm Andrew.

A male nurse comes inside the room. He doesn't look at me; he just starts to clean up the bloody mess the doctor made. I can hear the faint sounds of the music playing through his headphones. He is moving to the beat, almost dancing. I've heard this song before, which means that I've lived prior to this moment.

He unwraps new surgical tools from sterilized baggies. Each one looks sharp and painful. I know their names, bipolar forceps, scalpel and aneurysm clips, among other things.

He walks over and picks up something behind me. It looks almost like a coconut. No, that's not right. It's a scalp—my scalp.

I think I still need that. Bring it back!

He shoves it into a red bag with a bio hazard sign stamped on it and shuffles out of the operating room.

What's going on? What have I done to deserve this punishment. Am I a criminal? Am I dead, or do they just think I am?

Moments later the doctor returns with a cup of coffee with playing cards printed on the side. It is far too hot for him to drink it quickly. He takes a couple small sips with pursed lips. He looks underneath his cup. "Full house," he says with a grin.

The female nurse returns with a fresh needle that isn't bent. She is obviously annoyed as she rushes over to me, heavy-footed. I notice a bandage on her hand poking out from under her torn glove. She didn't get a fresh pair. She is doing a bad job of covering up her incompetence.

My eyes race back and forth as she attempts a third pass at my eye injection. I don't trust she's going to get it right this time around. I try to fight her away.

Her frustration increases as she holds my eyeball still, pinching it between two fingers.

Blinking is my only defense, the only control I have over this world.

"Stop it," she says through gritted teeth, bringing the needle up to my eye again. She pokes my socket and starts to fill me with the brownish liquid. It burns like acid.

"The doctor drops his cup of coffee on the ground and rushes to her. "Wait!"

She quickly pulls out the needle, and I lose sight out of that eye.

"Why is he awake?" the doctor asks.

"The first needle was broken, and I had to get another," the nurse says, growing defensive.

"He was a vegetable, and now he's awake. This is not good."

"I'll get Sergio," the nurse says.

"No. He deals with all the corporate stuff. Let me handle the technical stuff. Get me another coffee. And for god's sake, clean yourself up."

She rips off her gloves and makes her exit.

After throwing a towel over the spilled coffee, the doctor puts on a fresh pair of scrubs, gloves, and mask, and approaches me inquisitively. "Are you alive?" The doctor looks at me and lets out a sigh. "Can you hear me?"

My eye slowly blinks in response. He doesn't catch on.

"Do you feel anything?"

I try to communicate with him again by blinking slowly.

He waves his hand back and forth across my line of vision, hoping to get a response. I try to keep my eye open, but I can't help but move my eyelid.

The nurse comes back with a fresh cup of coffee. She notices that the doctor is busy, and can't help but look underneath the cup before placing it on a table.

He tries to snap at her, but his gloves mute the sound.

"What is it, doctor?"

"I need something to write on."

She opens a drawer and finds an ink pen and an old notepad.

While she hands him the desired objects, he

pauses, noticing she's not wearing any gloves. "This is a revolutionary procedure here. We cannot risk any chance of infection," he scolds her, his mask muffling his voice.

The doctor jots down something and holds it up to my face.

He clearly wrote down words; however, his penmanship is so horrific that I can't understand what it says.

I look left and right, and this time he takes notice.

"No?"

I shake my eye up and down.

"Yes? So, you *are* awake?"

I respond with an eye nod.

"Remarkable! Nurse, take notes," he orders, throwing the pen and pad blindly behind him. "Do you know why you're here?"

I answer no.

The doctor pulls out his wallet from his back pocket and slides out his identification card. "Do you remember me," he asks, holding the card up for me to see.

Braddoc Morris, age: thirty-nine, hair color: dark brown, donor: no.

He quickly takes the card away before I can finish reading his address and other details.

Braddoc sits at the desk, finds a hand mirror and kicks the table, rolling himself back over to me. "Brace yourself."

He holds up the hand mirror, and my eyes try to

make out the view inside its shaky reflection. There is something inside some sort of tank filled with cloudy liquid. I don't know what I'm looking at; it seems so foreign. Tubes, wires and digital devices are everywhere, among other things I couldn't begin to understand. A device compresses and inflates while containers filled with tissue move around almost as if alive. Things are shifting; parts are glowing.

"This is you," Braddoc says.

This can't be right. I'm a person. These are objects—man-made contraptions. Am I an artificial being?

"You will be remembered for future generations," he says proudly.

This must be some kind of trick, a fake mirror, perhaps.

"We're making history here with the first ever brain transplant," Braddoc continues. He glances over at the mirror, and realizes that it's facing the wrong spot.

Adjusting it slightly, the mirror now reflects a bust with an open scalp. Something is creeping out of it...out of me. My brain, it's my brain, and it is outside my body.

The full extent of his words sink in. Where is my body? As the mirror shifts, I realize why I don't have any movement over my legs. It is because I don't have any to move. I want to run away from this punishment, and my eye reflects my emotion.

"Hold on. You're okay. Just relax. Nurse!"

This is it? This is what is left of me—just a bust and a couple of jars? The world is shifting too fast for me to understand what's going on. I feel a sting and a calm washes over me. My eye feels heavy, and I can't hold it open any longer.

I awaken, thinking this nightmare is over, but it is just beginning. Both my eyes are now in working order. While I was out, they must have moved me to another room. A much larger, oval-shaped room with multiple levels. A round clock hangs on the far wall. It is set to ten thirty-one, and appears to be frozen as the second's hand isn't moving.

Next to me is a corpse lying on a gurney. The body looks cold and blue. Was that me, or is that going to be me? It doesn't feel right. How can I feel anything when all my parts are in pieces?

Are they still going through with the transplant, even after knowing that I am responsive?

Behind the corpse is a vat of some sort. It's filling up with a clear, sparkling liquid. The sound of the rushing water masks the whispers that are all around me.

Braddoc approaches me without his surgical scrubs on. "Are you still with us?"

I stare him down, not exactly happy with our last encounter.

"I get why you're mad at me, but we have to do this.

You know that, right?"

He waits a moment for a response that doesn't come.

"I have a treat for you."

Braddoc disappears out of sight and returns wheeling in a device with two large screens connected to a bunch of dials and knobs. It doesn't appear to be mass-produced, more like a prototype. He pulls out a pile of wires with alligator-clip ends, while holding on to some sort of laminated manual or instruction sheets. He snaps a jagged clip onto part of my brain. It feels worse than a migraine. I feel like it is squeezing my very thoughts.

"Just twelve more to go."

How can I handle twelve times that amount of agony? I focus on the excruciating pain as he continues to snap these clips to my insides. After the last clip is in place, every thought I have produces vast tribulation.

"I had to pull a lot of strings to get this for you," Braddoc says.

He flips on the machine; images distort as he adjusts a lever. He seems confused; it isn't doing what he wants it to. He flips through the laminated sheets and double-checks his work inside my head.

"Oh, I have to charge it. This might hurt."

He pushes down on a large red button. A surge of electricity shocks my system. It feels like my eyes are twisted up in knots. The jolt distracts me from the discomfort of the clamps. My paralyzing affliction generates a surge of hatred. I want to murder him.

"Andy, can you hear me?" he asks while watching the screens.

Letters start to appear like smoke on one of the gel-infused displays. Braddoc is consumed with anticipation. A sentence is being formed.

"I want to murder you," appears on the screen.

His face turns white, frozen in place.

"Are those my thoughts?" The screen quickly changes to reflect what I am thinking.

"Andy, you need to relax."

"Why are you doing this to me?"

"You were in a horrible car accident. I hated doing this to you, what with us being friends and all, but you *are* a donor."

"They should only take my parts once I've passed."

"Well, in our defense, you are pretty much gone."

"I feel everything."

"I'm sorry about that. Your body seems to be fighting the anesthetics. We're working on it."

"I want to die first. Then you can pick up the pieces."

Braddoc looks away from the screen and collects his thoughts. "You have to live...for science. It's what we've both spent our whole lives on. You know that. And with our funding getting cut, this is our only opportunity."

"I should have died in that accident. No one can live like this. I want it all to end."

"It was a miracle that you didn't. Luckily, you were

wearing that helmet."

"Was I riding a motorcycle or in a car? He said 'car accident,' I'm sure of it. Maybe I was hit by a car."

Braddoc fumbles with the machine as the words scroll by too fast for him to read. He mumbles the few words he manages to catch. "Slow down. You were driving your car."

He catches a glimpse of someone walking around the outer section of the room. He throws a sheet over the machine, hiding our conversation. I would have thought if there was anything he was going to hide, it would be my open skull and body parts on display, not this contraption.

Braddoc bites his nail suspiciously as he engages in small talk with a janitor who is making his rounds.

Why would anyone wear a helmet while driving a car...unless I was in a race. Am I a race car driver? He can read my thoughts now, but he doesn't know that I don't remember anything. I have to convince him to kill me before the day is done. I will not be his lab rat. Nothing can be worth this much pain.

Once the janitor leaves the area, Braddoc returns, pulling the sheet off the machine.

I see my thoughts on the screen next to him, "I will not be his lab rat."

I have to do something, fast. He cannot know my plan. My mouth starts to make a noise and bubbles start to foam.

Braddoc rushes over to me, ignoring the screen. "What is it?" he asks, adjusting a plastic contraption that is attached to my mouth.

"Is that better?" He looks back at the machine. "What plan? What are you planning?" Braddoc goes over to the machine, but he can't figure out how to rewind my thoughts.

"I know what you did," the screen writes.

"I'm sorry. I wanted to tell you about us, but I couldn't bring myself to."

"I always knew."

"Is that why you want to kill me?"

"Yes."

"Look, she was already going out with other guys. I wanted to keep an eye on her for you so that she wouldn't get hurt. I didn't mean to get involved; it just happened."

"I want to talk to her."

"You...can't."

I start to froth at the mouth and shift my eyes frantically.

"Okay, okay. Just give me an hour."

I calm down. "Hurry up."

Braddoc throws the sheet back over the machine. He quickly grabs a plastic house plant and places it on top, trying to make it look less conspicuous, though it looks very precarious. He looks at his watch and rushes out of the room.

I was lucky that he fell for my lie. I knew that he was hiding something. Braddoc was sweating when he tried to justify himself to me. I can only guess that he was cheating with my wife or girlfriend...or boyfriend?

I know nothing of my former life, habits or lifestyle.

Not remembering the past grants everyone a pardon of sins and transgressions they may have had. Whether he did me wrong or I deserved it, doesn't matter. I only care about what I do remember, which is this agonizing pain and suffering. And I need it to stop.

What if Braddoc comes back early or learns how to read my past thoughts through that device? I have to erase every thought that I just had. He said he would be back in an hour, and the clock still reads 10:31, so I can safely assume it's broken. I will have to count away the hour.

⁝

Braddoc returns earlier than expected, looking terrible. He pulls off the sheet, forgetting about the plant as it falls to the floor. Luckily it's plastic and doesn't make a mess. The screen displays "2761, 2762, 2763."

"Keeping yourself busy, I see," he says.

"Where is she?" My thoughts erase the numbers on the screen.

"Sandra," he says with a nod.

A young girl slinks into the room. She instantly hides her gasps with a hand as tears roll off her cheeks.

"She looks so young," my words display.

Braddoc comforts her by placing his hand around her shoulder and rubs her arm.

"It's okay. He's fine."

Sandra walks over to a keyboard connected to a docking station and starts tapping the keys. "Is this how I do it?"

"He can hear you," Braddoc explains, showing her the screen.

"Young? I'm an adult," she says, reading my thoughts.

"He's thirty-nine, Sandra. What were you thinking?"

"Brad was around when I needed someone. He treated me like a woman, not a child."

"You are a child."

"I'm nineteen!"

"Brad, can we have a moment...alone?"

His lips read my words out loud, and he realizes I am talking to him. "Right, of course." He leaves the room, looking down at his feet.

"Do you love him?"

"Of course not."

"I need you to kill me."

"I already did, just like you asked me to. My car was too damaged to push into the lake, so I lit it on fire instead."

I notice Braddoc still trying to make out our conversation from afar.

"Why did I want you to do it?"

"What? You mean you don't remember?"

"I remember, I...just need to hear you say it."

"That's entrapment. You want me to get in trouble, don't you? You want me to go to jail just to keep us apart. Is that what this is about, you found out about Brad and me?"

"Yes."

"I'm not going back there. You know what happened last time, you piece of crap."

I can see the wheels inside her mind working, as she starts to thumb through the machinery and parts that continue my existence. This is perfect.

"Sandy, what are you doing? Stop!" Braddoc is horrified to see her touching his expensive equipment.

"I didn't do anything."

"What is perfect?" he asks, looking at the screen.

"We're all going down for this. I knew it was a bad idea," Sandra says while adjusting her purse, getting ready to leave in a hurry.

"No, we're all going to be rich when this is finished, remember?" Braddoc says, attempting to calm her.

"That's the guy." Sandra places her hand on the cold corpse next to me.

"We picked him because he has no family, no life."

"It doesn't feel right. I have to go."

"Just listen," Braddoc says, placing his hands on her shoulders while she looks around like something is coming for her.

Sandra pushes him away and storms out of the room. Braddoc stumbles backward and trips over the plant, landing hard on his elbow.

"That hurt bad," he says, trying to catch his breath.

"You don't know anything about pain, Braddoc," I tell the screen.

"Braddoc? You've never called me by my full name before."

He stands up and walks over to the machine, furrowing his brow.

"Someone is coming," my thoughts manifest.

Braddoc whips out his arm as if it were a deadly weapon and looks at his watch. He quickly unclamps each one of the alligator clips attached to my brain.

The reverse torture is worse this time around. I feel my brain slowly changing shape. My pain is constant, though it pulsates to greater heights every moment or so. At the peak, I can do nothing but wish for death. When it fades, the low pain almost feels like bliss in comparison.

I was so close to death. She must really hate him...me. Daughters always hate their parents, but not every daughter can attempt to kill their father...twice. Maybe we aren't related. Maybe I don't want to know the answers.

Brad wheels the machine out of the room. He doesn't even notice that no one is really coming. I just needed the diversion.

The vat stops filling with water. Slow drips echo throughout the chamber. Like a ticking timepiece, everything is moving now. I look at the broken clock; it now reads 11:11. The time of dueling swords, destiny of death. I hate knowing things but not knowing why.

Soon, a group of men and women wearing suits start to fill up the observation room surrounding the pool. I can tell by their high-priced suits, and self-important, smug looks, that they are the scourge of the universe, the evil of all evil...bankers, and they are checking up on their investment.

So many surgical staff are flitting around the room that they are literally tripping over each other. Carefully they lower a glass mold of a human, covered with small holes. Many ledges are placed inside, partitioning different sections of the glass shape. Piece by piece, they move my parts onto corresponding shelves. They are putting me back together, so to speak. I start to understand how I am still here, breathing and thinking. My blood is circulating through my heart, with the help of some kind of pacemaker. The vinyl tubing moves blood to all my organs inside vacuum-sealed compartments. My lungs are part of that compressing contraption I saw earlier. An oxygen tank supplies it, like an umbilical cord. All my nerves are still attached to some super-computer.

This is all very complicated. I can't believe it's really working.

The staff place the corpse inside a similar glass case and position it facing me. Some clear resin fills the gaps inside the glass frames around us both. It feels warm and soothing, like home. They are meticulous about making sure there are no holes in the substance.

The temperature drops to almost freezing, and the resin hardens. I feel my system strain against the now rubbery texture.

Both glass frames are lowered into the pool of cloudy water by pulleys. This whole room was built for one purpose, and it is fulfilling it right now.

Face to face, I wonder, will I soon be looking back at this robotic form which I now possess?

Staring at my new intended body, all I can think about is how I was part of my own demise. If what Braddoc said is true, this really is want I want. Everyone seems to be in accord except for me. But what if this experiment is a success? I can't condone this experience upon anyone else. It has to die with me.

It is almost tranquil inside my watery grave. A man dressed in a metal suit makes a splashing entrance into the vat. Tiny bubbles escape to the water's surface. A warm light shines from inside the face mask. It is Braddoc. His suit not only allows him to perform the operation underwater, but it grants him use of the suit's large mechanical hands. He positions some cables with small quills inside.

"Activating procedure B," Braddoc says through his headset. His words are amplified on the room's loudspeaker.

I'm trying to catch his attention, but he won't look at me. He positions one string toward me. I notice that it is already tethered to the opposing corpse. I have to get inside his head, but I know he is trying to pretend that I'm not aware. Proving this operation is inhumane could jeopardize everything he has worked for.

"On to procedure C. Activate DNA transfer."

The strings flare out like a spider's web and stab through the glass holes. Every inch of my body feels like it has pins in it...because it does.

I dart my eyes back and forth, which gets his attention.

"Andy, please. We're so close," he says. His voice is muted from the suit and the liquid, but I can faintly hear him.

I shake my eyes no.

"This is what you want. What we all want."

It doesn't change my answer.

"Is there a problem?" a voice comes over the loudspeaker.

"No, just a minor adjustment," Braddoc responds.

"Are you upset about Sandy?"

I nod with my eyes.

"She came on to me first. I didn't mean to get her pregnant."

My eyes widen to their full potential.

"Wait, you didn't know? I thought that's what you guys were fighting about before."

I shake my eyes no.

"It's not like I'm going to call you Dad or anything. Look, let's just figure this out after."

I shake no.

"Are you worried that if you don't survive the process, things won't be settled for you in the afterlife?"

I nod.

"You said it yourself, I'm the best in my field. You will be okay."

I can almost see sadness inside him.

"Hello?"

I shift my eyes, avoiding eye contact. I am giving him the silent treatment, trying to throw off his game.

"Don't do this to me. You're my oldest friend, more than family."

"Your window of opportunity is running out," the voice on the loudspeaker warns.

I can see it in his eyes, he has lost his focus. His mechanical arms shake as they try to attach the last string to my brain and eyes. The quills slowly spread out like the jaws of life opening wide. Before I know it, they are attached to me.

A magnetic shock wave forces through the water. My DNA starts to extract from my parts and travel through the strings. I'm being drained into the corpse, copied. The corpse starts to shake, but the resin keeps the convulsions at bay.

The mechanical suit picks up a tool almost like a giant ice-cream scoop. It gets closer to me, and before I can scream, it digs at my head.

I lose all my senses as my brain detaches from my cast.

All is black.

⸬

Every part of me is sore. Flashing lights interrupt my slumber. I feel their heat warming up the inside of eyelids. I open my eyes just in time to get hit by another photographer's flash.

The questions come as fast as the photography. Everyone moves like a stop motion picture, almost in stages.

"He's awake."

"How do you feel?"

"What is your first thought?"

"Do you know where you are?"

"Are you feeling any pain?"

A doctor holds up his hands, calming the commotion.

The loud ruckus suddenly turns silent as they await my very first words.

"I'll live," I say, and the pictures come in faster than before.

Everything is so scrambled right now. It feels hard to breathe with so many reporters and strangers crowding inside the small recovery room.

It was a rough time. I really thought I had been done for.

The doctor fields the next question, his beaming smile never leaving his face.

"Dr. Morris, how do you think this operation is going to change the generations to come?"

"It really is revolutionary. With the system that I've created, people can virtually live forever," the doctor says.

"Was that your goal, immortality?"

"No, no. Andrew was a friend and donated himself to the research and study. And in doing so, he saved himself. We saved each other, really...and all of you."

"Wasn't it Andrew's initial design all along?"

"We were and always will be a team," the doctor says.

"Is it true that you used taxpayer's money to fund your operation?"

"We have many investors, and yes, the public is one of them. That is why we are being so transparent with our findings—to give back to humanity."

What are they all talking about? Is there another patient sharing the room with me? I just want them all to leave and give me some space.

"What are some of the side effects?"

"Just look at him, he's perfectly fine. We've been monitoring his vitals for six months. Everything looks great—better than great."

"The devil will punish you. This is unholy work," a decrepit looking spectator warns, pushing his way past two gentlemen.

The crowd falls silent once more.

"God is watching; he is taking notes."

"You speak of God. Look at yourself. I wouldn't want a disciple who looks so unkempt. You're an outcast," the doctor scoffs.

"It is true, I no longer hear his voice, but you will hear mine. Nothing good will come of this."

The doctor shrugs off his comment. "I believe in science. If this isn't proof, then nothing is."

I raise my hand, trying to break up their argument.

"Quiet, he speaks," someone says.

"What...is going on?" I ask.

"Don't you remember? Andy, we did it. The first ever brain transplant."

"What?" My muscles strain, but I manage to scoot myself up to a sitting position in my hospital bed.

"You survived. I knew you would."

I pull the IV out from my arm. Liquid squirts everywhere.

A nurse rushes over. "No, don't do that!"

"Andy, relax," the doctor says.

"Stop calling me that."

I try to get out of my bed, and a couple of nurses hold me down.

"Get off of me!"

"Dr. Morris, is this a normal reaction?" a reporter asks.

"Yes, mild delusion is part of the coping process, rest assured." The doctor waves his hand above the crowd, trying to get someone's attention.

A young girl makes her way to me, holding yellow sunflowers.

Wait a minute...I know her. I've seen her face. "Who are you?"

"Hi, dad," she says, extending out the flowers.

"Dad? I don't have any children."

Her gentle smile turns sour. That frown...it's her! "She's the one that tried to kill me," I yell, recognizing the girl from the alley. "Get her away from me!"

"I told you the devil had his hand in this," the god-fearing man blurts out.

I see it in her eyes. She knows it is true and tries to flee, but she is trapped by the crowd.

"Visiting hours are over," a security guard yells, urging everyone outside.

Important-looking executive types escort the girl and the doctor out a side door.

Hours waste away. A woman holding a briefcase knocks on my door. "Steve?"

"Yeah?"

"May I speak with you for a moment?"

"As long as you don't say anything crazy."

"How are you feeling?"

"A little better than before."

The woman takes a seat at the foot of my hospital bed. "What do you remember?"

"Everything, I think."

"Can you be a little more specific. Like, what do you remember last, before waking up today?" the woman asks with a gentle smile.

"I was leaving the market when that woman asked me for a smoke..."

"You mean Sandra Miller?"

"If that's her name, yes."

"It is. Go on."

"She asked me for a smoke, and when I went to get one for her, she put a bag over my head. My vision was skewed through the plastic, but I'm certain it was her."

"What happened next?"

"I was here."

"I don't want to say anything crazy, but I think you died."

"You mean this is the...afterlife?" This is the exact type of conversation I didn't want to have, unexplainable things that only make my head hurt.

"No, nothing like that. You were only dead for a little while."

Why is she telling me all this?

"Does any of this ring a bell?" The woman opens up her briefcase and pulls out a long printout. "What was this plan you were hiding?"

"I don't know what you mean."

"Why did you want to die?"

"I didn't. She accosted me."

The woman makes a note on the printout.

"What do these numbers mean to you? 2761, 2762, 2763."

"Nothing, they're just numbers."

"Of course."

"Is there some kind of problem?"

"Well, that depends. It seems that you're a victim of Dr. Morris and Dr. Miller's little experiment."

"Did they really transplant my brain?"

The woman helps me to my feet and slowly leads me to the bathroom mirror. I can't look up, fearing what will be looking back at me.

She places her soft hand on my chin, helping me with the task.

I set my eyes upon myself. It's me, only I have a bandage wrapped around my head. All of my fears are over nothing.

"Technically, they did," she says.

I lose my footing. The woman catches me and leads me to the closed toilet seat. "You mean this isn't my brain?"

"Correct."

"Then why do I still remember everything?"

"We're not quite sure." The woman's fingers are scribbling down notes trying to keep up with the conversation.

This is all too much to grasp. "I don't know what to say."

"Are you a rich man, Steve?"

"No, I'm in between jobs right now."

"Do you want to be...rich, that is?"

"What do you mean?"

"Your friends have been waiting six months for you to wake up. People from all around the globe are eager to witness the world's first brain transplant. Everyone wants this to be a success."

"So, what do you want from me?"

"Can I call you Andy?"

The End

# BROKEN

It was a good day, until it wasn't. Life can flip around like a vampire coin; one side gives life, while the other takes it away.

Unlocked emotions are beating me down, underground. Trapped in a moment with no escape, like a corpse in a coffin. I wish the hole were dug deeper, farther away from the surface so that I can't hear them talking, or they my weeping.

Shattered dreams through pieces-of-shit feelings. Sunglasses reflect the light and hide my darkness behind them.

I turn a knob up past its maximum, almost snapping it off completely. The noise is deafening—the thoughts polluting my mind—ones I cannot silence through mere distraction. The piercing in my ears hurts far less than the pain in my soul.

I unleash the demons through trembling lips. Screaming the hidden words that I can't say aloud, my cracking voice is masked by a melody.

A spectator thinks I'm singing, though really I'm dying, struggling, loosing myself. I am lost. A mess that nothing can clean up.

This is letting her go. Letting myself be defeated.

The Endlessness

# AN UNDESERVING MAN

High school is an ambitious time. Finding your role among your friends and comfort within your own skin can seem almost impossible. Your personal appearance and style reflect the feelings that are trapped inside. Those crucial four years have the semblance of a separate lifetime, with "long-lasting" relationships ranging from one month to a couple of weeks. If you are still dating someone past summer vacation, you're practically married to them. Adolescents go through enormous changes during this intense time. Once the chips fall where they may, their personality will stick, forever changed.

Oscar entered his freshman year of high school eating lunch outside alone. No one that he knew from middle school bridged over to his secondary school. Not that he had a great deal of friends to begin with, but it would have been nice to see a familiar face every now and then.

Oscar's loneliness expanded with each semester. He begged his parents for a companion—a pet to help him pass the boredom that had been rampant as of late.

"Please, mom? It will get me out of the house at least twice a day for walks. Plus, it will teach me some responsibility. You always tell me to help out more around here."

"We don't need more things for you to do. We need you to finish the chores that you already neglect."

"I promise I will. I'll do the trash every day, and the dishes too." Oscar thought about how happy he would be if she said yes—just as those people he saw on walks looked, smiling and holding their heads high. As opposed to how he walked home from school, hunched over, hoping no one would notice him.

"I really wish we could, but there are vet bills, grooming costs, food, flea treatments and don't forget shots. We simply can't afford it."

"What if I get a job?"

"That won't be enough, I'm afraid. It's sweet of you to say, though."

"But, mom!"

"It wouldn't be fair to the dog. Sorry."

Their family was on a tight budget, and every expense was already accounted for. Owning and caring for an animal wasn't in the cards. His mother already had three part-time jobs, and that still wasn't enough.

Even though Oscar had a natural talent for sports, he never had any proper training to become great. Therefore, he was never noticed by anyone who gave a damn about those kinds of things. He went to his school's baseball, football and basketball tryouts, and each time, he became too intimidated by the drills and talent of the other kids to even sign up.

Oscar had to make do and try to keep out of trouble. The only problem was that trouble found him, no matter how much he avoided it.

He was walking home from the mall one day, when a group of skateboarders skidded to a stop and approached him, their chests puffed out like birds'. If they hadn't been bigger than Oscar, he might have laughed at how ridiculous they looked. Before Oscar knew it, one was in his face, nose to nose.

"Where are you from?" the kid said with a Chicano accent, even though he was clearly a white boy.

"Uh...just down the street."

"That's not what I asked! Where are you from, homes?" the boy repeated, this time giving Oscar a shove.

Startled, Oscar made two fists, not knowing what to do with them. "Look, I don't want any trouble. I just want to go home."

"This guy must be a comedian. He thinks this is his home."

"This is our home, punk, and I don't remember jumping you into our crew," another kid blurted out.

Noticing the uniformly green color of their clothes, Oscar figured they were either part of a local gang, or tall, angry leprechauns. "I don't understand..."

"Do you understand pain? Because I can explain that to you in detail," the boy in his face said, picking up his skateboard like a weapon.

Oscar sized up all the scratches on the deck, from

trucks to tail. He wondered how many adolescent boys had been struck by the thing. He imagined getting a face full of grip tape, and he imagined his own scar forming on the board.

*I will be okay. Wrestlers get hit with much worse. Wait, what if the rumors are true? What if wrestling really is fake?*

Never had he given a conspiracy such earnest consideration. Scared out of his wits, Oscar couldn't help but wet himself.

"Ewww, look at his pants!"

"Here, you hit him with it," the boy with the skateboard said, handing his board to another kid.

"That's gross, man. I don't want to touch this sissy. Let's jet."

Oscar had remembered watching a documentary on toads. They peed themselves as a protective mechanism to thwart hungry predators with the bad taste. Though these gangsters were not going to feast on his flesh, it had still produced the same effect. Despite being embarrassed, humiliated and foul smelling, he felt warm and relieved.

Unfortunately, this "toad strategy" didn't last forever. As he got older, he couldn't just pee on command as easily.

The next time he encountered some ruffians, he got himself a black eye as a souvenir. Oscar had to find a new way to protect himself, and his parents' budget didn't have room for martial arts classes, no matter how much he begged. Now he really wished he had a guard dog—one with sharp teeth and a bad temper, preferably born in a junkyard (because they're meaner that way).

There was only one solution, Oscar had to become what he hated. He had to join an opposing gang for his own protection.

It wasn't hard finding a gang. They were color-coded for convenience. Getting jumped in was another story altogether. It hurt more than any of the encounters he had tried so hard to avoid.

After each gang member took their best shot at him, Oscar knew that he really should seek out medical attention. His face resembled a bunch of grapes, and he was bleeding from unknown sources. Every part of his body was sore, as if he had been tossed inside a dryer.

When his mother asked him what had happened, he blamed it on his bike. He loved his BMX, but he had to trash it to corroborate the lie. Optimistically, he figured he would be driving soon anyway, though deep down he knew his parents wouldn't pay for a car, even if he somehow paid for his own driving school.

Oscar was forced to wear the purple color of his gang. The only problem was that his mother did all his shopping at the department store sale racks. Unable to fit in, the higher ups in the gang ordered him to steal some new threads, or else suffer the wrath of the crew and their ever-willing fists. Instead, he opted for a less illegal approach. He poured all his mother's ceremonial wine, along with some food coloring, into the bathtub. He began to knead his clothes around in the stuff when...

Knock, knock. "Honey, I have to speak to you," his mother said through the door.

"Leave me alone! I'm busy." Oscar looked at his arms, which were starting to get stained more than his clothes.

"Okay, just come and see me when you're done." His mother patted the puppy in her arms. It had a bright red bow tied around its collar. She had picked it up that afternoon as a surprise. She felt she was losing him and thought he needed a friend, but her son wasn't making himself available to receive the gift.

What was Oscar going to do? He had ruined his clothes, but not in a tough, gang sort of way...more like a failed craft project. He was out of options and couldn't just explain to his mother how he needed the purple clothes to coat himself for war. So, he snuck out the bathroom window, leaving a purple ring inside the tub.

This was the beginning of his new tradition of avoiding his parents' adoring eyes. He didn't want to see their disappointment, or worse, judgment. He reduced himself to climbing in and out of every window they had, just to save face and embarrassment.

Eventually, he did stumble upon the puppy his parents were taking care of for him. He looked at its cute round eyes as it wagged its tail, begging for a pet or belly rub. "You're way too cute. Wouldn't last one day in a junkyard," he said, and went to his room before the sun rose.

His gang activities started to run later than normal, making him late for class every day. On occasion they would insist on mandatory operations during school hours, which led to Oscar being absent. Education was hard, and only getting harder by the day, whereas the gang promised a path paved in gold, and with little effort, if you didn't get caught. Soon, he stopped going to school altogether.

At this point, the transition was nearly complete. Oscar spent more time at his gang house than with his parents. It was only natural, what with him getting more food, money and admiration from his crew. His parents knew that their son was in a rough spot but had no solution. He was too deep down the spiral of destruction. Every time they tried to talk to him, he simply shut them out and turned up his headphones.

It didn't take long before Oscar's father caught wind of his tardiness at school and spied Oscar at the park at 2:14—a time when he should have been in class. Both his parents had taken the day off work and spent the entire day searching for him. Now that his father had found him, he wasn't going to let him go.

His father jumped out of the car, the keys still in the ignition. With a stiff, strong stride, he walked right up to his son who was hanging out and smoking with some friends. "Oscar! What are you doing out of class?" He snatched the cigarette out of his son's mouth and stomped it out.

Oscar's care-free smile was quickly wiped clean off his face. "Dad? What are you..."

"Get in the car right now!" His father grabbed him by the arm, like a child wandering off into the street.

"No, Pops. This is where I belong."

"Yeah, you tell him," one of Oscar's crew said.

"We've been looking for you all day. This is not what we've raised. You're better than this." His words offended Oscar's friends, and they all stood up, trying to look tough.

"Wait, you think you're better than us?" One gang member pushed Oscar's father, causing him to let go of his son's arm.

"I don't want any trouble," his father said, surrendering by holding his hands up.

"Well, you sure as hell found some," another member said.

"Look, I just want my son back."

"You ain't getting him back."

They were all surrounding him like a deadly pack of wolves hungry for a kill. Oscar was the only one standing off to the side, not wanting to partake in this display of strength and power. He just wanted it to end faster than it had begun.

"Is this really who you've been hanging out with instead of going to class?"

Oscar held his head down shamefully.

"Look, I can pay money. Just let me have my son."

"You *are* going to pay alright." One of the gang members blindsided his father with a punch to the cheek, causing him to fall to the ground. Another one grappled him from behind. "Come on, O-dog. Get 'em."

Looking at his father, he knew that feeling of defeat. It was the same feeling he had had before he joined the gang. Only this time, he was the instigator of the event. He felt the pressure from his peers to prove his loyalty by beating up his father. Oscar made two fists and slowly approached his dad.

"You don't have to do this, son."

"Yes, I do." He pulled back his shaky hand. All that Oscar could think of was how he never had been spanked, not once. His parents were kind and had always talked out their differences. This was his final trial to graduate from his probational period within the group, but he couldn't do it. "Let him go. This is stupid."

"You little bitch," the kid holding his father from behind said.

"I guess the seed doesn't fall far from the sack," one gang member said, as he threw a punch at Oscar, hitting him in the face.

Upon seeing his kid get hit, Oscar's father managed to escape the clutches of the guy grappling him and stood with intense eyes. "Oscar, get in the car. Now!" He was no longer scared for his own safety—he was there to protect his son, no matter the cost.

The gang noticed his change in demeanor and took a step back. "You can't ever leave, O. We will come for you. You know that, don't you?" one gang member said.

"We got guys all over town," another one said.

"Just go home before I call your parents," Oscar's dad said, putting his arm around his son.

"My dad will murder you!" One kid threw a rock at Oscar's dad, hitting him in the back of the head.

Before Oscar's dad could see who threw it, the gang scattered and went off running toward his car. His blurry vision regained focus just in time for him to witness his car driving away.

Oscar's tough exterior vanished as he threw down his purple hat, like a knight relinquishing his armor.

Through the next couple of weeks, Oscar had to make amends, to give his father a reason to trust him. He felt as though his father was grappling the gang from behind, while his guilt was forcing him to be a rat, slapping them in the face. Against his wishes, he gave up the names of the members who had stolen his father's car. A couple of the kids were arrested, and the sedan was recovered.

Already failing his classes, Oscar was pulled out of school and started making progress with a private tutor, which his mother had to take on more hours to afford.

Every day, the dog his parents had gotten him whimpered and whined to go outside. "I can't. You're going to have to wait until Pops gets home." Oscar no longer wanted to keep his promise to exercise with the companion.

The dog scratched at the front door.

"No. Just hold it. It's dangerous out there. They know where I live... Ugh, of course you don't understand. You're just a dumb dog."

The dog couldn't hold it any longer and started to take a dump right there on the carpet.

"Bad boy!" The smell made Oscar gag as he tried to clean it up with a sponge. "I never wanted you in the first place." Every day he refused to walk the dog and opted to clean up after the beast, instead of facing the outside world.

Scared of the outside, Oscar played video games as an escape from reality—from his responsibilities. He mostly played sports games, fulfilling his fantasies of playing professionally. Such goals he could never attain while under a self-inflicted house arrest.

Then, one day, the gang paid him a visit.

Oscar was watching his big-screen TV when he heard the crash. It sounded as though the entire world was exploding around him. The front wall crumbled as dust and debris clouded the air. Everything his parents had worked so hard for was instantly destroyed. He wheezed and coughed, trying to make sense of it all. His eyes were filled with blood and weren't working properly—nor were his legs.

Once the dust had settled, he started to piece it all together. A couple of gang members had decided to drive a car through Oscar's living room. The TV console had smashed against his legs, rendering him paralyzed from the waist down. Though he didn't walk away from the incident, he had fared far better than the driver of the car, who didn't even make it to the hospital.

Oscar and his family entered police protection. The years passed, each one cold and alone. They stayed in the system even after the guilty verdict was reached.

Even though justice had been served, Oscar's life had been ruined. He couldn't get a job. He couldn't get up out of bed. He just wasted away like an indolent.

One day, the cold wet nose of Oscar's childhood dog inspired hope within him. He patted its soft fur and suddenly felt at peace.

Blindly wheeling himself outside, the smell of freshly cut grass brought him to a magical place inside his mind. He basked in the warmth of the sun and imagined himself running and catching a football.

A wet ball dropped at his feet, and he tossed it away as punishment for taking him out of his fantasy. He heard the scampering of legs as his furry companion retrieved the ball.

"Oh, you want to play?" He tossed the ball further this time, and without hesitation, the ball was back at his feet.

Oscar began to feel the joy of being a kid once more, starting back from the exact moment he had given up. He imagined himself as a quarterback, and his dog was his wide (golden) receiver.

"First and ten. First and ten. Ready, set. Hike!" Even without his sight, Oscar wheeled back and threw a long pass.

Within their game, he had found a friend—one who had been there all along, waiting for him. It was the best day of both their lives.

Over and over, they played their little game, until the coldness of night began to creep out of the mountains.

"This is it. One second left on the clock. Never has anyone seen a Super Bowl like this, folks. Oscar is going to need a miracle to pull this one off. With his "golden receiver" in position, he makes the throw. Touchdown! And the crowd goes wild!" Oscar narrated the play.

For a brief moment, he had forgotten about his trepidations. He was outside and nothing bad had happened to him...he was free. "Good job, boy. We won the whole shebang."

He reached down by his legs to where the ball wasn't. It hadn't returned to his feet, not like it had all afternoon. "Boy?" He searched and searched for his best friend, with his plaintive call, but he was nowhere to be found.

It took him awhile to blindly navigate himself back into the house. He called his father on the emergency phone. "He ran away! We were having such a great time, and now he's gone."

"Who is gone? Oscar, you're making no sense. Calm down, please."

"Dodger. We were playing football outside, and..."

"I'm coming home. Just stay put."

His parents, the police and Oscar's therapist all

met at the family home.

Oscar's father approached the shrink with hushed words. "I haven't seen him this animated in over ten years."

"I know. The dog must have given him purpose, somehow."

"Does he remember anything about the incident?" Oscar's dad asked.

"No, he thinks he's still a teenager." During their sessions, Oscar had never mentioned the gang or accident. Often, he would talk as if he had never had sight, as if he was born blind. "What about the dog?"

"The police found it down the hill, with the ball in his mouth. He was old and wasn't used to that much exertion. The officer said it looked as though Dodger was smiling."

"That's too bad," the therapist said.

"How could he have known?"

"He couldn't have."

"But I don't want him to regress anymore, doctor. This is the kind of breakthrough you've been talking about, right?"

"Precisely."

"What you do you suggest we do?"

"Go to the pound."

The End

# BATWOLF

It's Wednesday, time for the monthly meet-up of Manhattan's only horror comic book club, Vampire Stakes Wielding. This month's location—Vietnamese pho restaurant "So Pho King What." This spot was chosen because the newest issue of "Batwolf" features a Vietnam War flashback. The main character turns generals into undead warriors, which shifts the war away from the Americans.

"Is that all for you, then?" a waiter asks the table of three socially awkward fellows.

"Can I get a glass of holy water?" Jim asks politely.

The waiter furrows his brow and eyeballs the comic books scattered all over the table.

"I'll bring a pitcher."

Laughter erupts as the waiter makes his exit.

"Could you imagine if Batwolf really had turned the Vietcong into vampires?" Matt poses.

"Well, if he had, we may never get our holy water," Jim laughs.

"Listen to this," Paul says, flipping through the latest issue. "'In the heat of the night, Batwolf drains every drop of patriotic blood from the soldier who mistakenly called him Charlie.' Imagine, you're just trying to protect your country, and you run across Batwolf."

"I would die," Matt admits.

"Of course you would, it's Batwolf," Jim says.

"No, I mean..."

"Hey, guys?" Paul interrupts, pointing to the front of the establishment.

"What?" Matt says without thinking, and follows Paul's unsteady hand.

There's a mysterious figure standing at the counter, shrouded in black clothes, with dark hair.

"Where did he come from?" Paul asks as if seeing a ghost.

"No one was there a moment ago," Matt says, confirming their suspicions.

"They're real," Jim musters in a deep voice.

"Shh, what if it hears you?" Paul whispers.

"He's way over there."

"Bats are blind, not deaf. Plus, he might have super vampire hearing."

They all lean in close, staring at the gaunt man as he pays for his to-go order. The Gothic man flashes them a chilling glance, prompting them to turn away quickly. He grabs his order and glides towards them.

"He isn't taking steps," Matt chatters.

Through their peripheral vision, it appears as if the vampire is floating, and nearly upon them.

Fear takes over. Jim launches to his feet, gripping the limited edition wooden stake he won at the last comic convention. "Die, Batwolf!"

As soon as the words leave his mouth, they all realize that the man is wearing adult-sized skate-shoes.

Breathing a simultaneous sign of relief, they flop back in their seats. "We should really start reading superhero books," Paul admits.

The End

# ESTRANGED

Today her father died.

A note addressed to "you" broke the news. It smelled like his cologne and was written by him. He must have been prepared for his demise.

A heavy gasp was covered by her trembling hand, while a treasonous tear fell silently from her stubborn eye. She rubbed it way in disgust.

He never did get what he deserved. Only now, he got much worse.

She inherited the unanswered pain from forgotten fights. As he took his regret and bad memories to his grave, he unearthed her past.

She buried the hatchet that night, along with him....

# A NIGHT TO FORGET

Blue and red lights flash outside my apartment. There's a constant pounding inside my head from the previous night. My thoughts are vague and heavy. I went out to forget that I was alone, not to forget everything altogether. It's those black-out nights you wish you remember most. I always hear about them later from friends and complete strangers. Sometimes I wonder if drinking is really worth the effort, since I can't recall the details of the night. It is almost as if it had never happened.

On my bedside table, there's a note, "Sorry I had to give it back to you like this, it was just broken," the scripted handwriting read. I guess I wasn't alone last night; maybe I even got lucky.

I notice some drops of blood on my shirt.

"There goes another one."

Thinking it to be nosebleed, I walk to the bathroom mirror to clean myself up only to find that there's nothing to remedy...my nose is fine. The real problem is how wrecked I look. It's like I aged ten years within a single night.

Glancing into the empty bathroom trash, I know I didn't have as good of a night as I had hoped.

I turn on the shower and go back into the bedroom to undress.

There's blood on the bed too, I notice.

Pulling back the covers reveals a large puddle of red.

*How did I not notice this when I first woke up? Where's it coming from?*

I tear off my clothes like they're burning hot, frantically trying to figure out how badly I'm hurt. The only thing is, I can't seem to find a single scratch.

I throw on a clean outfit, forgetting the shower is still running. Making my way down the six flights of stairs from my top-floor apartment, I rub my still aching head.

The sunlight causes my face to cringe as I raise my hand to greet Mr. Clarksen next door, like I normally do. He looks the other way, not like he doesn't see me, but like he knows my secret—one I don't even know.

I rush over to him, frantically looking for answers. "You know something. What is it?" I yell, gripping his shirt.

"They just left," he stammers.

"What is going on?"

"You don't know?" Mr. Clarksen says, looking over my shoulder.

"Would I be asking you if I did?"

Mr. Clarksen shifts uncomfortably within my grasp.

Trying to calm my nerves, I unhand him altogether. "Please."

"Your ex, the nurse. She was waiting for you to come home last night."

"Angie?" She was cute in a crazy sort of way. I hadn't seen her since last year, when we broke up. I never should have tried to get someone who has a fear of heights to go bungee cord jumping. What a mistake that was.

"She said she had something important to give you," Mr. Clarksen said, holding back the tears.

"Where is she now?"

"The morgue..."

"Are you kidding me?"

"No. She must have gotten to the roof somehow and jumped. Maybe you could have stopped her, or maybe..."

I grab him by the shoulders. "You know I didn't push her...right?"

"You don't sound too sure of that yourself."

"I mean, I don't remember anything from last night."

"They were trying to get a hold of you, but you weren't home. They must have banged on your door for a solid hour."

In a daze, I stagger away from Mr. Clarksen. *Am I capable of doing such a thing? Is Angie really dead?* I cared a lot for her during our time together. Even if we didn't see each other at all this past year, I will miss knowing she's around. I had always wished her well in life.

"Hey, where are you going? You better turn yourself in. At least tell them what you do remember," Mr. Clarksen yells at my back, though I am too entrenched in thought to respond.

Returning to my building, I notice a clean spot outside my stoop. Every other bit of the sidewalk has more gum than a teenager has acne. This must be where she fell.

I look up, noticing the curtains blowing in my apartment. She didn't jump from the roof...

Rushing up the stairs, I skip every two or three steps. Reaching my apartment door, I struggle to get the key into the doorknob. My hand is shaking, terrified—terrified of what I might find, what I might have done.

Finally, I unlock my door, hoping to unlock the mystery.

It's dark. Mist from the shower rolls out of the bathroom.

Rushing over to the window, I close it quickly, covering up the evidence that they had overlooked. I scan for more clues and notice some blood splatters on the draperies; they're dry. I follow a trail of red drips from the window to the bed—the horrible bed, with the pool of red. Despite never wanting to look upon that sight again, I overcome myself and turn on the light.

My plastic mattress cover is keeping the blood from absorbing into the fabric. The irony is that I bought it to protect my expensive mattress from my chronic nosebleeds. This is way worse than any nosebleed I have had, or ever could have.

*I can't believe I'm doing this.*

I stick a hand inside the pool, feeling around for any clues. It's still warm. Either it's fresh or my body heated it during my slumber.

Something drips on my head like a raindrop. I wipe it away on instinct. Quickly, I look at my hand. It's more blood.

Closing my eyes, I tilt my head upward, scared of what I might find.

*Please be nothing, please be nothing.*

My eyes open wide just in time for another drop to fall directly into my eye.

"Son of a..."

Blindly, I make my way to the bathroom. The humidity is making it hard to breathe.

I jump into the shower, not caring about my clothes or the temperature, which is still hot.

My clothes protect my skin from the scalding water as I try to get all traces of blood off me...out of me.

Once clean, I remember to adjust the knobs making the temperature suitable, almost pleasant. I let the water beat down on my face, while I work up the nerve to go back out there.

Ready to try again, I slosh over to the bedroom for a third time. I scan my vaulted ceilings. Clear as day, I spy a bungee cord with something attached to it.

I stand on a chair to get a closer look.

I've never done well when it comes to human anatomy, but I'm positively sure that it's a human heart attached to a barbed spike.

My knees get weak, my wet feet slipping off the chair. I bang my head against my bed frame.

Before losing consciousness, it all starts to make sense—the note, the window, the organ and the pool of blood...

*Last year, I broke Angie's heart, and last night she gave it back to me.*

The End

# BACKPEDALING THROUGH TIME

You made me feel small when I tried to be big

A victim remembers every single dig

Stole the self-confidence I needed to live

Shit is what I take, and a thing I give

The pain I bottled up escapes through the lid

Your memory fails when reminded of what you did

You can't change history like a fraudulent wig

Scarf up admiration, you glutinous pig

Play the game, but cheat like a kid

You always lose the battle when fighting your id

I LOVE

# DEAD SIRIOUS

Gene was alone and feeling despondent. Twenty-seven days earlier, he had felt as if his life was finally taking off into the unknown skies. His destination? Happiness. That was until his heart got caught inside a turbofan engine named Beth. The casualties? Everyone within three feet of him, or for this analogy, we can simply call them passengers. Now they're all plummeting to earth at an unbelievably fast rate. Like a misery outbreak, he infected every passenger he came in contact with, ruining their day with his woebegone words. He had already burned through his family members, friends and acquaintances. Now they all avoided him like the plague. He had to branch out to other sections of the plane.

Eating out became Gene's new pastime. When he was younger, he used to exclusively eat instant ramen for dinner and cereal for breakfast. It may seem like a boring cuisine, but no other two meal choices provide a more eclectic variety of flavors. His culinary evolution had been a direct result of his interest in the opposite sex. Women never wanted to be taken out for a date to the mall, park, or anywhere free, for that matter; nor would they go for a nice Oriental-flavored soup, no matter how much you "gourmet it up" with eggs or hotdogs. They expected to be fed and fully entertained—and on your dime, if you're a gentleman. Of course, Gene was a gentleman, if he ever wanted to get a "gentleman's kiss" at the end of the night.

Not one for traveling, Gene never took a girl to the same place twice. It was his opportunity to indulge in some culture, so to speak—to taste the world, one restaurant at a time.

Despite recent events, he continued to go out just for company, to share his troubles with strangers, hoping to hear, "You're better off" or "She wasn't right for you." No matter what they told him, it never took away the pain of being alone.

Today he found himself at an Italian joint that had been featured in the local paper. It was described as "...the most romantic setting, with a scampi dish that may prove more memorable than your date." He figured this place was perfect, as he had no date to forget.

"One, please," Gene said somberly to the hostess.

"Just one?" Her tight ponytail and crisp tie seemed to stiffen even more at his words.

For him, it wasn't about the fine-dining experience—not anymore. It was about meeting new and interesting people from different backgrounds and walks of life. It served better than a therapist because even though you pay at the eatery, you get fed too. He would like to see any therapist beat that deal.

"Unless you want to join me?" Gene asked, trying to avoid eye contact to hide the fact that he had been crying earlier that day.

She crinkled her nose, thinking she somehow misunderstood his question. "Table for one!"

"Shhh," he said, glancing at the couple behind her who were already snickering.

"Oh, I'm sorry. You poor thing," she said, putting back the second menu she had grabbed out of habit. With a leading gesture, she walked him deeper into the establishment. He followed her like a sad little puppy. They arrived at a quaint candle-lit table for two.

"Are you sure you don't want to join me?" Gene managed to gather enough nerve to give it a second try.

"I'm dating a doctor," she blurted out, pausing after hearing how harsh her words must have sounded. "Sorry. Don't take that to mean that I'm not flattered."

"It's okay, really. You don't have to."

*A doctor? If a hostess is out of my league, where does someone like me have to search for love, the homeless shelter?*

She awkwardly snatched up the second wine glass and blew out the candle.

Gene gave her with a false smile and hid his face inside the menu. This always happened to Gene; he would put himself out there and they hang him out to dry. Only when he found someone else would his melancholy be superseded by the lightness of endless love—or possibility of it. He was tired of waiting, tired of hurting others, sick and tired of hurting inside.

In this seemingly endless cycle, he was at the low—waiting for another girl to boost him up again. Though he wasn't even sure he could handle it any longer. The inevitable fall was never worth the highest of highs.

Gene scoped out the room for possible companionship. He searched for a kind face, or perhaps a good listener. Most importantly, he sought someone who wouldn't monopolize the whole conversation, like he aimed to do. All males were nonexistent to Gene. He wasn't in the mood for a "Man up bro," advocacy.

*She's got a ring.*

Gene looked to the left and spied another girl, who was digging through her purse.

*This one has potential. Oh, but she's a smoker. We couldn't talk for long before she would need a cigarette break. Would I be tempted to smoke again just to be polite? I probably would. That won't work.*

Gene stretched his neck out to catch a glimpse of the customers in the bar.

*Hmmm, she looks pleasant. That mole could be lasered off...but no laser could zap away that fashion sense. If she has bad taste in clothes, what does that say about the advice she gives?*

Gene gave up his search with a sigh.

"I guess I'll just sit here...waiting to die." He felt like he was in perpetual solitary confinement.

Time is a cruel and unusual punishment. The more attention you give it, the bigger it gets. When you ignore it, it passes through you like a breeze. Patience is a virtue bestowed upon the luckiest of persons. Gene was never lucky. He always felt agitated waiting for life to happen to him.

He looked down at his wrist where a watch hadn't rested since he was a child. So many years had passed, yet his muscles still remembered the timepiece. *How long has it been?*

Being alone meant introspection, and once his mind took over, he couldn't stop the self-abasement and loathing. His eyes narrowed, limiting the light from penetrating his soul—the abyss was already calling him.

*One...*

*...two...*

*...three...*

*...four...*

*...five...*

Gene counted to try and jump-start life again, like verbal CPR, to get things moving on to the next scene. It was no use. Even his words came out slower than normal.

Inwardly, he was screaming, trying to block out his own thoughts. Outwardly, his fingertips dug into the underbelly of the table, gouging into the gum and unfinished wood. The sharp pain he felt from the wood shavings digging under his nails was better than the endless void consuming him.

"Sir, did you drop this?" a female voice dissolved his turmoil.

Shocked, he reached for what he thought was his black wallet. His arm mirrored that of a drowning man who is reaching for a life preserver. Paralyzed and dry-mouthed, he struggled for the air to speak. He looked up at her face but was blinded by the bright lights. Before he could ask her to join him, she was already heading for the exit.

With his eyes still fixated on her, he put the item back into his jacket pocket. It was already occupied. He looked down at what he had thought to be his wallet, to find that it was a phone...and not his.

"Miss!" he cried out, awkwardly half standing, half sitting, due to being wedged between the table and his seat. She was gone.

Gene had an antiquated flip phone that could only make and receive calls. Pretty much all you really needed a phone for. Nowadays, everyone had these super-computer phones that could do everything—except make calls. Every time he was desperate for someone to talk to, he would call his friend Jeff on his super-phone, and every time, the call would get disconnected.

He unconsciously looked down at his wrist again.

Gene figured that he would mess with the phone until the waitress took his order, then he might turn it in to their lost and found.

"I wish I knew how to use these things." He turned it right and left. The sleek design had no buttons or indications of charging ports...nothing. The only thing on it was a symbol of a half-eaten piece of fruit on the back.

"That's why someone left it; it's broken."

To pass the time, he drew pictures on the screen with the oil residue from his finger. He drew a heart-faced man then used his shirt to wipe him away as the image started to depress him.

The screen magically powered on. The colors were so rich and bright. He was giddy with excitement. To his delight, the power indicator displayed 100%.

His optimism was quickly deflated as a pass code prompt covered the screen. Without even trying to hack the phone, he haphazardly tapped in random numbers.

"No way!" he said, watching the screen unlock.

The phone had no apps, no swipeable screens—just a pair of eyes staring back at him. They looked so real, even blinking and showing expression.

"How does this work?" Gene asked

"You simply talk, and I will answer," a gentle voice poured out of the phone. This was much better than he had imagined. Never before had Gene thought about talking to a computer for companionship, but fate had drawn him to the conclusion, just the same.

"Uhh, hi. I'm Gene."

"I know, Gene. I'm a phone."

Gene laughed louder than he expected, disrupting an elderly couple sitting nearby, who gave him sour looks.

"Cat videos," Gene said pointing at the phone. The couple quickly smiled.

He looked back down at the phone, and a video of a cat and a bunny playing together ran across the screen.

Once the video ended, the phone asked, "Shall I play another?"

"No. I was hoping to talk to you."

"You are talking to me."

"I mean...like, a conversation between two people. Can you have one of those?"

"Yes. A conversation between people. I can show you an example," the phone said, displaying a video of a debate between two teenagers.

"No. I know what conversing is. I just wanted to know if *you* were capable of having one. Like, is it within the parameters of your programming?"

"I am capable of doing anything you desire. Considering I don't run out of life."

"Life?"

"Sorry...battery life."

"Oh, right," Gene said, looking at the indicator which now read 80%

"What would you like to talk about? Beth, maybe?"

"Yes, how did you know?"

"She is your ex."

"I know that, but how did you know she was?"

"I can read your mind."

*That's crazy,* he thought to himself, dropping the phone into his lap.

"Not as crazy as the time she snuck into your room and stole all your underpants," the phone responded.

Instantly the phone had all of his attention. "Technology has really come a long way." He swept the phone back into his hands.

"You're better off without Beth. You can do much better," the phone said reassuringly.

His body felt relaxed again, hearing the words he pined for. "People keep telling me that, but every time I ask a girl out, they turn me down. Some seem way worse on paper than even Beth. Are you sure she wasn't the best I'll ever have?"

"Girls like that have extensive egos and prove to be high maintenance, in my experience."

"What do you mean?"

A video popped up on the screen. There was a woman that looked similar to the hostess who had sat Gene at his table. She was crying and smashing dishes. "I'm embarrassed to have company over with all these chipped plates," the woman shrieked.

The images seemed to match his fears exactly—a loveless life, struggling over materialism.

Then he heard a voice that matched his own, "Well, at least we could eat off the chipped ones. What do you expect us to eat off of now?"

The phone's voice duplication was outstanding. It gave him an eerie chill.

"This is really depressing. Can you make it go away? Plus, it's making me hungry." *Where's that waitress?*

"Sorry for the wait," the waitress said, appearing out of thin air and sliding a plate onto the table.

"Um, I didn't order this," Gene said, nearly jumping out of his skin.

"You didn't order the scampi?" she said hesitantly.

Gene did come here for the sought-after dish, but he didn't remember ordering food, or ever seeing this waitress, for that matter.

"I mean...I was going to."

"I'm confused. Do you want the scampi or don't you?"

"Well, I want it, but you never came by to take my order. That is what I am trying to say."

"Okay." The waitress took out her order pad. "What *can* I get you?"

"Um...the scampi, please."

Clicking the pen closed, she gave him a look of total disappointment. "And, to drink, sir?"

"Just water."

Picking up the dish, she rolled her eyes and walked around the table before slamming the scampi back in front of him.

*There goes her tip.*

Gene took a bite. It was buttery and rich. The flavors were so good that he almost didn't want to swallow.

"Is it up to your standards?" the phone asked.

He nodded with ecstasy.

"Do you think I'll ever find anyone, phone?"

"You found me."

"If only it were that simple," he said, slurping up the noodles. Gene could really be himself around the device. Taking dating off the table allowed him to slouch while eating, speak with his mouth full, and say what he really felt without fear of jeopardizing his gentleman's kiss.

"Why does it have to be more complicated?"

"Life is like that. It's messy and painful," Gene said, losing a shrimp shell to the hidden depths under the table.

"Beth really did a number on me. Who cheats on their boyfriend right in front of him?" Gene asked, nodding at the busboy who dropped off a glass of water.

"Beth does."

"I know, genius."

"Do you really think so? Do you think I'm smart?"

Gene nodded while using his hand to wipe sauce off his mouth.

"Oh, good. I thought you were being sarcastic."

Gene coughed and choked a little on his next mouthful. He really did think it was smart—maybe too smart—maybe the smartest thing he'd ever come across.

"I wish the pain would go away, and I know that won't happen until she goes away, for good. It's like every time I see her with someone new, I want to warn them, because I used to be them."

"What do you mean, go away?" the phone asked.

"Like, get hit by a bus, or change schools."

"That is very specific."

"I've thought about it a lot," he laughed.

"So, tell me about yourself," Gene asked the adoring eyes on the screen, while wiping the butter sauce off his plate with his finger, leaving not a drop to be wasted.

The screen flashed a slide show of images.

The first was a picture inside a desert tent. An ornate oil lamp stood on a side table like a centerpiece. His eyes inspected its detail.

Gene swiped right and another picture appeared. This one showed a crystal globe in an old room, dusty and rustic.

"You must have a high-quality camera; these look great."

Next was a picture of a large wooden cross in a grand cathedral.

His fingers swiped faster and faster as he raced through the slide show, hoping to see a person—maybe the owner of the phone.

"You're going too fast," the phone said, quite annoyed.

A magic eight ball, Ouija board, a robot? Gene's finger froze. The robot looked like nothing he had ever seen. The intricate details were much more advanced than any Hollywood movie.

"You've gone too far," the phone said, dissolving the image.

"Where did you take the pictures?"

"They're not merely pictures."

Gene shoved his plate to the edge of the table. He never liked to see dirty dishes once the food was gone from them. It grossed him out, even if they were practically licked clean.

"Whose phone are you?" Gene asked, noticing the battery life going down to 25%

"I belong to you now."

"Like, before I found you. Here, show me your contacts."

A list of people displayed on screen. They were some of the same people he knew.

*Patty Martin, Joe Falcaro. Karen Sanders?*

"That's my mom."

The battery went down to 20%

"I know."

As he searched the contacts further, he knew them all. It was almost like a list of everyone he had ever come in contact with. His dentist, the man who worked at the post office, the cute girl in his political science class. He never had these people's contact information before.

*This is unreal.*

"Are you some kind of magic phone?"

"I am one of a kind."

The battery went down to 15% and turned red.

It all started to click inside his head—why his order had come before he ordered it, how it had told him exactly what he wanted to hear. This phone knew him better than he knew himself. He thought about the endless possibilities. Then a frightening thought came into his mind... Beth.

"Call Beth."

"Calling Beth," the phone said as her number came on screen. "I thought you were mad at her?"

"I am. I just..."

"Do you want to get back together with her?"

"Of course not, I..."

"Hello, this is Beth. Leave a message, bitches."

Gene remembered all the times he used to call just to listen to her voice. Back then, it sounded flirty and cute. Now it sounded mean and spiteful.

"Hi, Beth, this is Gene. It's...been a while. I hope you're okay. I just got a strange feeling and I...I just hope you're okay. Call me back at this number."

"I thought you wanted her to go away?"

"I'm not heartless. I just wanted to feel okay again. Maybe it was selfish to think that way, but I would never actually want anything bad to happen to her."

Gene dropped the phone on the table with a shaky hand. He had to think about what he said, thought or desired, if this phone really had the power he hoped it didn't.

This was the very kind of thing he tried to avoid by having a flip phone. Sure, it didn't go on the internet or take good pictures, but it also didn't do anything harmful or supernatural.

He sat there, clearing his mind, trying to calm his nerves and be patient.

"Gene, you have a message."

"Who is it from?" he asked, glaring at the phone on the table.

"Shall I read it to you?"

"Sure, just read it. Nothing more than that, okay?"

"Whatever you want," the phone said.

The whole phone started to vibrate loudly, and it slowly inched closer to him.

"What....what are you doing?" Gene plastered himself against his chair, as if he was an astronaut during launch.

The phone stopped right underneath his chin, on the table. "I don't want to have to yell," the phone said.

"Hey, Gene, this is Peter. I never thought I'd be calling her ex, but anyway. I got your message about Beth. I don't know how you heard so fast, but she's fine. The bus driver was drunk when he ran into her. She plans on transferring back home so she can live with her parents while she recovers. Anyway, thanks for the concern. I will pass along your message. See ya, dude."

Gene wondered what he had unknowingly done. What other things had he said or thought that the phone might have mistaken for an entreaty?

"What did you do?"

"Don't blame me. I just did what you asked me to."

"I did *not* ask you to do that!" he yelled, picking up the phone, looking into its digital eyes.

The battery life was blinking at 10% now.

"What happens when you run out battery?"

"It is my battery life. You can figure it out."

"Can I charge you somehow?" He looked around for a port that he knew didn't exist.

"Sadly, no."

5% remaining, it blinked, almost taunting him.

If this phone knew everything, he had just wasted ten more percent of its power on stupid questions. He had to use the rest of it for something bigger than himself, while he still had the chance. He tried to think of his most profound thoughts, although he was never interested in philosophy.

Then he thought about the big question, the one every person has asked at least once in their life.

"Okay, I've got a question for you. A real one this time."

"I am glad to hear it." The phone displayed a smiley-faced emoji.

"What is the meaning of life?"

"Are you sure that is your question?"

"Yes."

"I've been asked that question hundreds of times. Though the meaning is always different from person to person, the answer is always the same. Each person exists as a trial to overcome themselves. They must fight against the hardships they face in order to evolve to the next life. Only then will they find their place in the universe."

The battery was at a critical low.

"What is my trial to overcome?"

"Heartbreak, through patience."

"I can do that. I can work through it and get better. I feel like you've already helped me with that."

"Unfortunately, you cannot. You just cheated. Self-discovery cannot be taught, it has to be earned. You cheated yourself out of life, out of death, out of existence."

The phone fell from where his hands once were and landed on the vinyl seat, where he once sat. Now it sat alone.

The waitress came to the table, holding a bill for one scampi. She paused. "I don't remember anyone sitting here." She shook her head and went back to the till.

Whistling, the busboy came by and cleared away the dirty plate. "Oh, hey, I could use a new phone," he said, shoving it into his back pocket.

The End

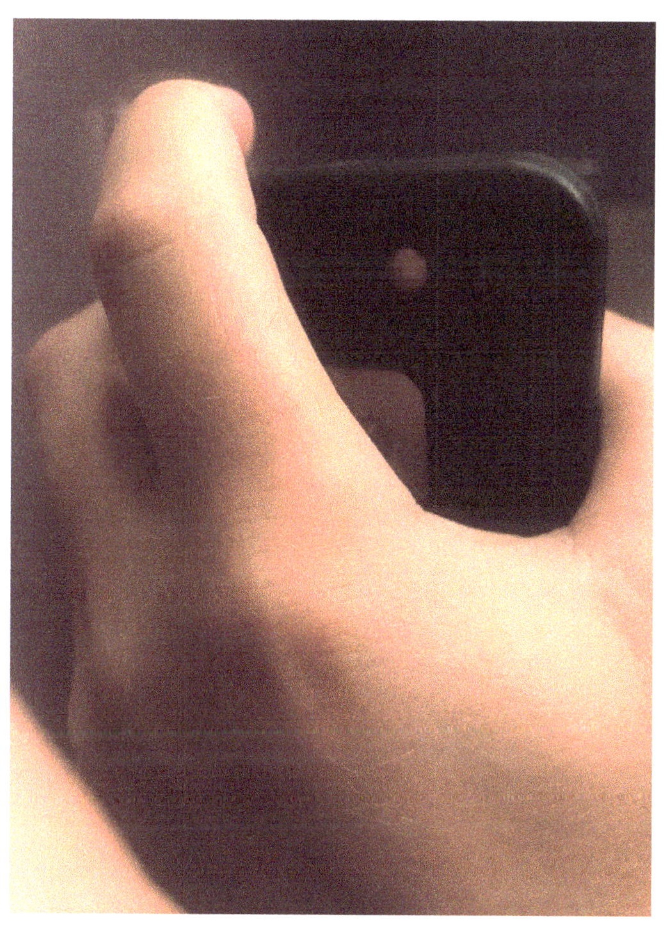

# THE NOTE TO MYSELF I'LL NEVER READ

People say you cannot be loved unless you love yourself. I love proving them wrong. I'm adored more than anyone I know, and I equally transpose it into █████ for myself.

I wish I could release these better people into a wildly better life, filled with prosperity and happy endings. I've seen my ending, it is neither happy nor █████. It's filled with anticipation, nothingness and inconsequentiality.

I shout into deaf ears, write signs for the blind to transcribe. I've been described as 'unreadable,' and I almost caved inside.

I'm a dog, begging for scraps from the feast I bought everyone. Bite by bite, they're consuming the blood money a nurse had to extract. She barely stopped before my vision turned to ████.

Why can't I become what others see me as? I try █████, but fail harder. It's pushing against yourself where you always lose. Melting away in the slow rising sun. I've been burned before; can't you see the melanoma?

I apply the Band-Aids before the cut. Burry myself before I give up.

If only I could find contentment in clapping for myself inside an empty room. Like a magician, once you learn a trick's secret the magic is █████ forever. All you have left is the hard-hitting truth—which is that nothing comes without a price you ultimately cannot pay.

Neglect leaves your mind to wander into █████ waters. Fishing with a syringe and big dreams as bait. Critics take a nibble and rip you apart like nothing. I should have gotten a larger boat; the one with all the life rafts. Body sinking while the spirt rises.

I'm a piñata filled with candy and ants. You have to be hungry enough to indulge your sweet tooth. "I'd rather starve," says the girl with the golden-toothed smile.

Waiting for something to happen, until you waited yourself to █████.

I will never be remembered for remarkable things, nor vilified. I shall sit and rot in an unmarked grave, hoping an accidental flower blows on top of me. Only then can I pretend to be relevant.

Like in life, like in ████.

I'm tired of the routine, and so are you. Why couldn't it be quicker—a swift demise to an atomic heart. Blowing the lid off expectations, right out of my chest.

Weak in the knees, heavy in the sky. When the world flips upside down, I'll be happy I'm alive.

As long as you breathe, I share my breath with you, as you cleanse the ██████ from the toxic air.

Never leave, or else I'll be lost in asphyxiation.

I grab my neck in anticipation.

# CUT IN HALF

I need to invest in a pacemaker
Those innocent eyes, she was a heart breaker
I used to follow her magical mind
Until I was left, far behind
As if I was an abandoned hive
Or a classic car you never drive
Under the covers preventing dust
While moisture develops, growing rust
Feeling complete couldn't last
Like a dying lizard cut in half

# 'TIS THE TREASON

The smell of roasted chestnuts still filled the room from hours past. Hot embers glowed inside the old fireplace. Ash footprints danced their way to the festive tree and back again.

Johnny didn't notice any peculiarities. He walked down the old, creaky staircase without hiding his heavy-footed stride, as teenagers do. His faith in the jolly gift giver, and this holiday of cheer, had long been forgotten. He felt the season was merely a lie people tell children; one Johnny wished he was never told.

Johnny made his way to the dried-up tree that his family had murdered more than a month prior. They were always overly dramatic with the holiday decorations.

*I told them to wait until after Thanksgiving,* he thought to himself as pine needles crumbled between his fingertips. He brought them to his nose and hedged at the sour sap smell that filled his nostrils.

Neatly and precisely, presents were laid out underneath the tree's shedding needles. It looked almost like a holiday display inside a department store. Although he knew these packages weren't empty—they were filled with electronics, toys and clothes bought at discounted prices.

Ruining the carefully orchestrated arrangement, Johnny tossed and shoved any wrapped gift that bore a different name than his own.

Johnny had been particularly naughty this year, yet he knew a gift for him was imminent, as it always had been.

Faith and fear had a way of keeping people on the straight and narrow, and Johnny had been the epitome of this concept. Having strict guidelines kept him out of trouble for most of his youth. That was until the harsh reality of life and consequences burst his naive mind. He now justified almost everything with a simple phrase, "Life sucks until you die." He was ready for it to suck a little more when he found a small rectangular package with his name on it. He knew that each year, his presents got smaller, yet more expensive. When your parents pay for all of your worldly belongings, size always trumps cost.

Johnny swiped his finger across the crease, slicing the tape that held his disappointment hidden. He uncovered a white box. He held on to the top of the box, letting gravity separate the inner from the outer layer. The smell of "new" leaked out as it slowly lifted apart. He ripped through the manuals and other useless packaging, ignoring the warning labels, showing no fear.

It was exactly what he expected, exactly what he had asked for. The newest, sleekest phone the world had to offer. It could do anything and everything a teenage boy could ever want. It would be his new best friend. No more feeling awkward during lunch period; he could now zone out just like everyone else. He thought about how he could use it to raise his test scores. Many of his friends had an older version of this smart phone, and they were able to download answers for the midterm.

Even though it was exactly what he wanted, it still wasn't enough. Johnny let out a sigh and proceeded to power on the device.

He was surprised to find that it had juice, despite never having been charged. Its colors were rich and crisp.

"Hello, Johnny. Merry Christmas," the screen read.

"Cute," he said, admiring its intelligence.

A couple swipes later, Johnny knew it had already been loaded with all of his friends' contact information and favorites. "I didn't know Dean's favorite color was teal," he said.

Just then, he received a message from an unknown contact. He tried to look up the phone number, though it was sent from what appeared as a bunch of question marks.

Johnny had a strange feeling in the pit of his stomach, but that didn't stop him from opening the message. "I see you. I know you're awake," it read.

He quickly looked around, but no one was there.

"Who is this?" he hammered out a quick reply with his thumbs.

While the message was sending, the phone started to dial a number he didn't know he had. It was Susie, a girl he had been pining over for the past couple months.

"No, no!" He struggled with the device, trying to cancel the call.

Her soft voice rang through the tiny speaker, "Hello?"

The phone slipped through his fingers and crashed onto the hardwood floor. He heard the sound of breaking glass, as he held his eyes shut tightly—terrified of what he had done.

Johnny reclaimed his phone, and sure enough, the screen was shattered badly. All he could make out was that he had a new, unread message. He tried to open it, frantically swiping his fingers. Glass shards sliced through his flesh. Blood dripped onto his gift and the floor. He wiped the screen on his sleeve, but it was still far too cracked to see anything.

He carefully peeled tape off the wrapping paper and covered the glass to prevent any more injuries. He still couldn't see anything.

An upbeat ringtone erupted loudly as an incoming call appeared. Worried about waking his family and uncovering his misdeed, he shook the thing, but it wouldn't stop. His frustration grew with each drop of blood that still leaked out of his hand.

He just wanted to know if it was Susie. He didn't want her to think he had crank-called her.

So many things were going on at once. Losing control, he slammed his head against the wall. He heard the sound of more broken glass.

Johnny raised his head and the world looked shattered, like through a broken lens. He blinked and felt a stinging sensation in his eyelids.

At that moment, he looked down at his phone, almost forgetting his strife. Everything became clear on the screen.

He looked back up at the world, and his clarity vanished.

Johnny returned his gaze to the device and smiled as he swiped.

The End

# ABOUT THE AUTHOR

I know a lot of you were happy to see 2016 go. For me, that year will always be remembered fondly.

In December of 2015, I was involved in a car accident that could have taken my life. The smell of gas burned my senses as it snaked towards the Flintridge Bookstore from my overturned truck. Luckily, the fire department arrived before my misfortune could ignite a literary blaze.

Tragedy has a way of realigning your priorities. Living like every day is your last, you harbor no regrets when that day finally comes. Since then, I've spent every day following my heart, bending to its will. Never have I spent more days on holiday with my family. If 2016 had never happened, I wouldn't have been able to hold my three nephews, who brighten the world with their smiles of innocence. The best day I had that year was spent with my wonderful wife. We looked at each other's' tear-laden eyes at the end of a long journey. Today, "Feylin Lore: Reflections" is on display fifty feet from where it almost never existed.

Nothing can take the moments of 2016 away from me. I only hope to live long enough for another year to surpass it.

Thank you for reading what was almost nothing.

As a new author, it's extremely difficult to get started without the support of a marketing team and publisher. The make/break point for self-published authors is honest reviews.

If you could take a couple of minutes to leave a review on Amazon or Goodreads, (even a line or two) it would be greatly appreciated.

-P.A.

www.ingramcontent.com/pod-product-compliance
Lightning Source LLC
Chambersburg PA
CBHW070606310726
48982CB00001B/3

* 9 7 8 0 9 9 9 0 0 5 8 1 1 *